AN EYE ON THE WORLD

AN EYE ON THE WORLD

Margaret Bourke-White, Photographer

BEATRICE SIEGEL

Frederick Warne
New York London

To my dear Aunt Naomi

Frederick Warne & Co., Inc.
New York, New York

Library of Congress Cataloging in Publication Data

Siegel, Beatrice.
  An eye on the world.

  Bibliography: p.
  Includes index.
  SUMMARY: A biography of a woman renowned for her photographic interpretations of war, revolution, and poverty and for her personal battle against Parkinsonism.
  1. Bourke-White, Margaret, 1904–1971—Juvenile literature. 2. Photographers—United States—Biography—Juvenile literature. [1. Bourke-White, Margaret, 1904–1971. 2. Photographers] I. Title. TR140.B6S58   770'.92'4 [B] [92] 79-2432
ISBN 0-7232-6173-3

A Selection of the Junior Literary Guild

Printed in the U.S.A. by Maple Press
Book Designed by Meryl Sussman Levavi

CONTENTS

ACKNOWLEDGMENTS

I would like to express my gratitude to Roger B. White for his generous help and for permission to use family diaries, letters, and photographs. I would also like to express my appreciation to Ralph Ingersoll, one of Miss Bourke-White's editors and friend, for reading the manuscript.

Others I would like to thank are: Sean Callahan, editor and author, who gave me the benefit of his personal experiences with Miss Bourke-White; Theodore M. Brown, Professor of Art History, Cornell University, for a lengthy interview; Carolyn A. Davis, the helpful guardian of the Bourke-White Collection and Manuscript Librarian, The George Arents Research Library, Syracuse University; and Susan Kismaric, Assistant Curator, Department of Photography, Museum of Modern Art, New York.

Thanks also to photographer Ann Cooper, a research resource, and my husband, Sam Siegel, who undertook the role of research assistant.

And finally I would like to express my appreciation to the family members, schoolmates, and colleagues of Margaret Bourke-White who kindly drew on their memories of past days for this book.

BEATRICE SIEGEL

ON CAMERAS

By Morris Engel

Though the cameras Margaret Bourke-White used at the beginning of her career are still in use today, they bear little resemblance to the small, easy-to-handle instruments most of us know. Today, the latest miniature candid cameras are completely automatic, and some even have automatic focus. They use a roll of film that can give 20 or 36 pictures and permit the recording of any rapidly moving subject. In the 1920s, however, these technical advantages were not available.

Margaret's first cameras were large and their operation required slow and painstaking steps. First, Margaret had to select and compose the subject. Then, she had to determine the exposure, set the shutter speed and lens opening, and focus the lens under the dark covering cloth needed to shut out the light. Finally, she would insert the film holder (each picture was made from a single sheet of film), remove the slide, and release the shutter. The slow speed of the camera required the use of a tripod (a three-legged stand) which held the camera steady.

Margaret's basic cameras were the 3¼ and 4¼ (film size) Speed Graphic, and the Linhof. She also used a light Soho Reflex, a heavy Graflex, and a 35mm Contax. When on assignment, she added to these cameras varied focal length lenses which permit different-sized images, wide views, and close-ups. She also needed large supplies of film and flashbulbs. It made a substantial load of equipment.

In the decade of the 1930s, Margaret added to her arsenal of equipment newly-developed compact cameras. These small cameras permitted her a greater flexibility of movement in the demanding subjects she photographed, especially during World War II.

Margaret was continuously confronted with decisions: which camera to use, and which lens, whether to use a flash (and if so, a single or multi-flash), and whether or not to use a tripod. At the same time she had to decide questions of even greater importance, such as: who, what, where, when, and why to photograph. These questions had to be quickly answered.

The camera gear that Margaret carried around created many supply problems. She was a prolific "shooter" with many cameras in constant use.

Margaret's work is ample evidence that she solved most of her problems. It was perhaps good timing that the photographic improvements in cameras, film, lenses, and flash equipment coincided with her own development.

Margaret Bourke-White understood cameras, both the larger and smaller ones. Her talent was so great that she made remarkable photographs with the early, slower cameras. The newer, faster ones gave her even greater range and freedom.

*   *   *

MORRIS ENGEL is a well-known photographer and filmmaker. He and Margaret Bourke-White knew one another at the Photo League in the late 1930s, and both worked at one of the landmark newspapers of the 1940s, *P.M.*

AN EYE ON THE WORLD

OF TOADS, SNAKES, AND BUTTERFLIES

Through the long night Margaret sat on the edge of her chair, her eyes fixed on an overturned glass on the windowsill. All summer she had collected caterpillars and lined them up under glass jars. In books on insects she had found out what these caterpillars ate and had fed each one a diet of its favorite leaves. She had watched the caterpillars change into the next stage of growth, enclosed in a firm case called a chrysalis. Earlier that warm September day she had noticed a slight wriggle in one of the chrysalises. Now, joined by her family in the all-night vigil, she waited. Occasionally she

Margaret at 11, holding a baby robin while the father robin feeds it

3

glanced over at her parents and her older sister, Ruth, also sitting patiently on stiff-backed dining-room chairs. Only her two-year-old brother, Roger, seven years younger than Margaret, was still asleep in his upstairs bedroom.

"Look," Margaret shouted when she saw the chrysalis split open. Then, completely absorbed, she sat through the long, slow process and saw a wet, curled up, shapeless insect slowly pull itself out of the chrysalis, stretch and smooth out its wrinkled wings, and become transformed into a full-blown beautiful butterfly.

Not only caterpillars interested Margaret. She brought home toads, damp pieces of tree bark encrusted with strange eggs, and jars filled with insects. Her favorite pet was a boa constrictor her father had given her as a gift. She knew it was a harmless snake. So was the old puff adder that sometimes lay curled up in her mother's lap when she sat reading newspapers in front of the fireplace. But friends and neighbors who dropped in to visit often shrieked in fright when they saw so much wildlife scattered over the dining-room floor.

Even before Margaret learned to read and write in the neighborhood school, her parents taught her to love everything in nature. She never saw them deliberately crush the smallest insect. A bee buzzing around the house would be caught in a glass and carefully freed outdoors.

Her parents had in common a love for nature. And they both came from poor families that had settled in the United States in the mid-1800s. In many ways, though, their ancestry was very different. Her father, Joseph White, was of Polish Jewish origin, and her mother, Minnie Bourke, was Irish

At one, Margaret looking out at the world

Protestant. Her father had been brought up to believe that faith in people was more fundamental than faith in God and therefore he never practiced his religion. Every person, he was taught, was worthy and deserved to be treated with respect and dignity. His parents, Margaret's Grandmother and Grandfather White, were active in the Ethical Culture Society in New York City, where such ideas were discussed and fostered. Her maternal grandparents, the Bourkes, were more conventional church members. Grandmother Bourke thought Minnie "was going to the devil" because she did not observe the Sabbath.

Joe White and Minnie Bourke met and started their courtship in Central Park during the early-morning bird walks. Then they rushed off to daytime jobs. At night they both attended school. Joe White was studying engineering at Cooper Union and Minnie Bourke was going to Pratt Institute to learn stenography, a desirable skill for women in those days. On Saturdays or Sundays they would pedal off on their bicycles to spend the day in the countryside. Margaret's father was even then a silent man, his head full of ideas for new machines. Her mother, lively and outgoing, filled the silence with enthusiastic talk about everything around her.

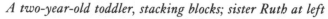

A two-year-old toddler, stacking blocks; sister Ruth at left

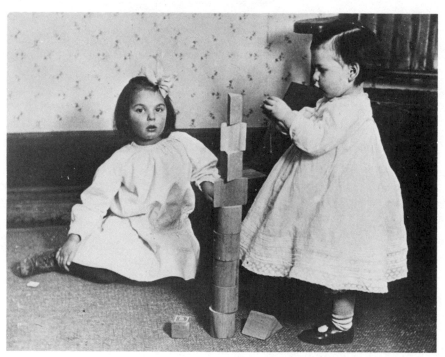

AN EYE ON THE WORLD

Brother Roger at work in the garden

After their marriage Minnie and Joe White remained in New York, and Margaret was born there in June, 1904. A few years later the family moved to Bound Brook, New Jersey, to be near the printing plant where Mr. White, now an engineer and inventor, worked.

Margaret grew up in a large house surrounded by trees and open fields. Within walking distance were the woods and rolling hills of the Watchung Mountains. In that lovely rural area Margaret found excitement in each season and every change of weather. On cold wintry days, when the snow glistened on fields and mountains, Margaret and Ruth, sometimes with brother Roger in their care, would go coasting down the mountain slopes. Or they would ice-skate on a

OF TOADS, SNAKES, AND BUTTERFLIES

Margaret climbing up to join Ruth

frozen pond. In the spring, Margaret brought home bunches of wild flowers and put out bread crumbs for the song sparrows. She used a good part of her free time to help plant and weed the vegetable garden. During summer vacations, her mother taught her and her friends how to cook and how to sew. There were always the walks to the library with Ruth when they challenged each other to a balancing match on the thin edge of a high wooden fence.

But nature walks with their father, when Margaret and Ruth could coax him out-of-doors, were unforgettable adventures. He could call birds to him by imitating their song.

AN EYE ON THE WORLD

Margaret's father, Ruth, and family pet Rover

And he taught the children how to pick up harmless snakes. By the time Margaret was ten years old, she dreamed she would become a great authority on snakes, a herpetologist; she would travel to the jungles of foreign lands for rare species "doing all the things that women never do." Above all, she knew she had to travel, like her Irish ancestors whose sons had run away to sea.

While Margaret's father was gentle and smiling on their nature walks, he was very different at home. Most of the time, after dinner, he would work at his drawing board. Or he would sit in a living-room chair sunk into a deep silence, unaware of the family tiptoeing around him. Even when Margaret's mother asked him a question, he might remain silent. The question hung in the air like a puff of smoke. Sometimes, a week later, he would answer it.

"He's a perfectionist," Margaret's mother would explain, trying to help Ruth, Margaret, and Roger understand the father who sat in their midst but yet was in another world. "He's trying to solve an engineering problem," Margaret's mother would say. Sometimes on one of those rare occasions when the family ate in a restaurant, Margaret would see her father push his food aside and draw sketches on the tablecloth.

Margaret often watched her father. She adored him; and it pained her to see how hard he worked, to see his face become grim and stern and to know she could not penetrate the wall of silence that surrounded him.

Early in the marriage, Minnie Bourke showed the strain of sharing a home with her withdrawn husband. "If only he would talk more," Margaret would hear her mother complain of her father. Her mother had the full responsibility of the large house and three growing children. And if Margaret's father was a perfectionist, her mother also set high standards for herself and the children. She firmly believed that time had to be put to constructive use. From morning to night she was busy in the home and in the community. (Later on she would take college courses, study braille, and become a devoted teacher of the blind.) Though the family was well off and could afford many comforts, Mrs. White had only the occasional help of a gardener, handyman, and seamstress. She kept a watchful eye on ex-

*Margaret's mother, posed and photo-
graphed by Joseph White*

penditures and could account for every penny in the same way she could account for every hour. With that same vigilance, she educated the children to meet her high ideals.

"Reject the easy path! Do it the hard way!" she drummed into Margaret with her ABCs. When Margaret came home from school after an exam, her mother would say, "I hope, Margaret, if there was a choice of questions, that you answered the difficult ones and not the easy ones."

"Tell the truth," was another daily lesson. "Margaret, was it an accident or carelessness that you broke the soup plate?" her mother would ask when a plate shattered to the

OF TOADS, SNAKES, AND BUTTERFLIES

floor. She forgave an accident and punished carelessness, but none the less expected a truthful answer.

Growing up in a large rambling house surrounded by trees filled Margaret with terrors of the dark and of being alone. She clung to Ruth when she thought she heard strange sounds during the night. To help Margaret face her childhood fears and overcome them, Margaret's mother took the situation in hand. She made Margaret comfortable with a favorite jigsaw puzzle or book and left her alone in the house, at first for five minutes and then for longer stretches of time. One day Margaret discovered she had spent four hours alone in the house and had actually enjoyed the solitude. To help her handle her fear of the dark, Margaret's mother devised another game. She made Margaret walk partway around the outside of the house in one direction as night fell. When Margaret was about to scream in fright, she would find her mother coming from the opposite direction with outstretched hands. Margaret learned that nothing sinister lurked behind the maple trees. In fact, she began to enjoy the outdoors in the dark.

Even Margaret's handwriting received her mother's full attention. For her eleventh birthday, Margaret received a gift from her mother with a note:

Dear Margaret:

If you will practice writing in this book every day or at least five days each week during vacations, and your handwriting shows improvement by September 30th, you may make out a list of surprises, one of which you would like as a reward.

Your loving Mother

AN EYE ON THE WORLD

P.S. It would be a good plan to choose a sentence for each page, and write it over and over until the page is filled....

Margaret's penmanship did improve and in meticulous handwriting she started the first of many diaries the year she was eleven. Her mother made her understand that no matter what her experiences and feelings were they were valuable and worth recording.

Each day Margaret felt challenged to meet her mother's demands and win her approval. She worried when she thought her mother might hear false tales about her. "I was trying to be as nice as I could tonight but Grandmother [Grandmother Bourke was visiting at the time] and Ruth were cross," she wrote in a note when her mother was out.

When Margaret and Ruth fulfilled their mother's expectations, she rewarded them with a special treat. She took down from the book shelves a heavy volume they called "The Family Medical Book." Together they pored over diagrams and charts of muscles, bones, and blood vessels. By the time she entered high school, Margaret had learned the mysteries of the human body and how babies were born. In many ways she was more advanced than her school friends. She had so many things on her mind that sometimes she would sit in the classroom and stare out the window. She could be thinking of the baby robin that had fallen from its nest and that she had rescued. She had worried about what to feed it when one day, sitting on the lawn with the tiny robin in her lap, the father robin hopped over with a worm in its mouth to feed the chick.

Even if at times her mind wandered, she was so bright

OF TOADS, SNAKES, AND BUTTERFLIES

Elementary school graduation class; Margaret seated on grass, left

that she quickly learned every lesson she was given. She excelled particularly in writing. When she was only fourteen, in her second year in high school, she entered the writing competition open to students in the upper classes and won the coveted prize for "excellence in literary composition." Her excitement at winning the prize—three books she se-

AN EYE ON THE WORLD

lected for the cash award of fifteen dollars—was dimmed by an experience later in the week. At the senior class graduating exercises in the school auditorium, the principal called Margaret to the stage and handed her the books. Afterward, when the auditorium was cleared of chairs and converted to a dance floor, she proudly stood around, confident that her winning an award would make her popular. She loved to dance and would waltz around the kitchen at home with a dish towel draped around her. Her mother, who always seemed so wise, would say, "If you are a good dancer you will always get dancing partners." But it did not work out that way. That evening in the school auditorium, Margaret, tall, slender, with lovely deep blue eyes and abundant dark hair, stood alone along a wall of the dance floor, hugging her heavy books, a bright smile on her face—and not one boy asked her to dance.

What was wrong? She straightened her dress and patted down her hair. She watched the boys line up and wait for other girls to be free, while she stood along the wall clutching her prize books: the *Frog Book*, the *Moth Book*, the *Reptile Book*. She continued to smile even though a hot flush of embarrassment was creeping up her cheeks. Finally, an older girl, a friend of her sister's, whirled her around the dance floor. She stumbled through the dance, positive everyone was staring at her. In those days girls did not dance together in public.

Though Margaret yearned to be popular and to have dancing partners, she was never an intimate part of a school group. When classmates gathered together and laughed over something ridiculous in a comic strip, or at a light movie, or even about the latest fad in chewing gum, Margaret would not know what they were talking about. Her mother would not allow comic books in the house. Only rarely was she allowed to go to a movie. She was not permitted to chew gum, play cards, use cosmetics, wear frilly clothes, or do anything her mother considered silly and useless. She could not even visit classmates who had comic books in their homes.

Margaret had a few close friends but, cut off from light amusements, she struck most students as "different." The boys considered her too serious-minded to invite to a dance. On the other hand, deeply involved with her own life, Margaret often did appear distant and reserved. Sometimes she had the air of a superior being looking down on her classmates. "My home is in heaven, I'm here on a visit," was the comment one classmate made of her. Still, the students respected her and elected her class president one year. She made the swimming team, went on canoe trips, and played basketball and hockey. No one could deny her competence and her bright mind. She had a great store of information and could easily roll off the names of Greek gods; she knew classical music as well as classical literature. She put her knowledge and her marvelous facility with words to use when she became an editor of the Plainfield High School senior class book, the *Oracle*. With another editor, John Daniel, she wrote appropriate and witty comments under each graduate's picture. She told her best friend, Charlotte Luf, whom she called Tubby, that she and John were writing a poem for the class book, and in lofty tones Margaret recited a sample verse:

AN EYE ON THE WORLD

"We're starting on the Road of Life,
Unconquered lands before us lie
Where each one hopes to find success;
But how we hate to say goodbye!"

The highlights of Margaret's growing-up years were the occasional Sunday visits to the factory with her father. There she would see the rotary presses he had invented, which had brought about a radical change in printing, making possible a continuous printing process. On one memorable day her father took her to a foundry where the parts for one of his machines were being cast. She climbed up to a sooty balcony with him and looked down into the dark depths. She would never forget the thrill of seeing the sudden burst of flying sparks and flowing metal that lit up the pitch blackness. Margaret was beside herself with excitement.

Not only printing presses but cameras, lenses, prisms, and the magic qualities of color engaged her father's inventive mind. Margaret would laughingly pose with the family while her father experimented with different lenses. Though cameras were lying around the house, Margaret never took a picture in those days. She would casually pick one up and examine it, but cameras held no interest for her. Nevertheless, familiarity with cameras became part of the legacy from her parents along with hard work habits, perseverance, courage—and an enduring love for nature.

OF TOADS, SNAKES, AND BUTTERFLIES

THE GIRL WHO TAKES PICTURES

When she graduated from high school, at age seventeen, Margaret had no great interest in a specific career. Science was important to her, and teaching was a possibility. Teaching had become a popular profession for young women going on to college. But the arts also absorbed her. At Rutgers College, which was only twenty minutes from where she lived, she took courses that summer in dancing and swimming. In the fall she entered Teachers College, Columbia University, and started the long daily train trip to New York City. Enrolled in the Practical Arts division, she took the usual first-year courses in biology, French, and drawing. But to add to her knowledge of design and composition, she signed up for

The library tower and clock, Cornell University, 1926–27; one of the photographs Margaret sold for a dollar to help meet expenses

a class in photography with Clarence H. White, a lecturer in Fine Arts at Teachers College. For the class, her mother gave her an Ica Reflex camera for which she had paid only twenty dollars because it had a cracked lens.

Clarence H. White was a man of worldwide reputation whose work hung in museums in both the United States and Europe. An associate of the great photographers Alfred Stieglitz and Edward Steichen, he offered his students an appreciation of photography as a fine art and as a way to express beauty, while leaving the practical instruction in shooting and developing pictures to an assistant. White worked on his own prints with various chemical processes and paper to achieve a "soft focus." His scenic studies and portraits are distant, moody, and shadowy—they look as if they had been shot through a mist.

To take the class in photography, Margaret traveled the short distance from Teachers College on West 120th Street up to West 144th Street, where Clarence White ran his School of Photography. There she also listened to guest lecturers and picked up odd bits of knowledge from other students, many of whom, like Ralph Steiner, were starting distinguished careers of their own. Margaret would say in later years, "The seed was planted with that course." Dorothea Lange and Laura Gilpin were also among the outstanding photographers who took classes with Clarence White in their early years.

At the end of Margaret's first semester at college, her father died. Though grief-stricken over their loss, Margaret and her family had to face hard problems. Mr. White, always a dreamer, had made no provisions for their financial care. Margaret offered to leave college and look for a job, but her mother made it clear that she expected the children to continue with their educations. Somehow they would manage, she said. Uncle Lazarus White, her father's brother and also a successful engineer, remained close to the family. He tried to complete an invention for a new color printing process Margaret's father was working on at the time of his death, but the details were too obscure. He was able, however, to advise the family about financial matters and help with the children's education.

Margaret knew now that she had to earn money, and that summer she put to use her knowledge of photography. It qualified her for a job as a counselor in a children's camp in Connecticut. She taught children how to take pictures and how to develop them in the darkroom she had set up. But she completely enchanted them with her knowledge of wildlife. One evening when the children were especially noisy, she jumped up on a table and told them the exciting story about "the beauty sleep a caterpillar takes and wakes up more beautiful." On nature walks she would show them a garter snake, and to their amazement and delight, she would pick it up and explain the difference between harmless and dangerous reptiles. She made pets of two snakes, and soon the children were freely handling them. They collected every bug and wild flower and brought them to Margaret as if they were precious gifts.

During a three-day hike to the top of a high mountain, Margaret took pictures of its rolling slopes. She had already shot pictures of Lake Bantam, where the camp was located. When the camp directors saw the scenic beauty Margaret portrayed, they asked her to print two hundred picture postcards for sale to visiting parents.

After she saw the children off to bed, Margaret rushed over to the darkroom. Night after night, with the assistance of another counselor, she printed the cards.

When most of these were quickly sold, the directors ordered another five hundred cards for the following season. To earn additional money, Margaret took a sample of the cards to town and convinced several gift shop owners to offer them for sale. By the end of the summer she had orders for over a thousand cards. "I am so proud of myself. I feel as if I can make my living anywhere," she wrote in her diary.

To fill the orders, she stayed on in camp after the children had departed. It was a lonely time, and the days dragged. Her friends among the counselors had also left, and even though the kitchen staff was helpful, she spent almost all her time alone in the darkroom, doing each card by hand. When finally she had hung the last print up to dry, she figured out she had made almost two thousand cards that summer.

Margaret was glad to leave camp behind her and get back home to Bound Brook. Her brother, Roger, was away at boarding school, but she, her mother, and Ruth had a joyous reunion and stayed up half the night talking. Part of their discussion concerned Margaret's return to college.

They were trying to figure out how, with their limited funds, they could manage it. But the problem was resolved a few days later in an unexpected way. A wealthy family in town, who had set up a fund for worthy students recommended by high school teachers, offered to put Margaret through a year at the University of Michigan. "I'm really going back to college," an elated Margaret reported to her mother.

She repacked her belongings and set off for Ann Arbor, Michigan. There she shared an apartment with three other young students. During registration, she signed up for science courses, certain she was headed in the right direction and would become a biologist. Still fascinated by herpetology, she took a special course with the noted authority Dr. Alexander D. Ruthven.

The days when Margaret had no dancing partners were long behind her. Tall, lean, her dark hair cut short, and glowing with energy, she had a deep, warm sense of "belonging" to the university. She moved through her days as purposefully as an arrow heading for its target. She worked hard at her courses, went out on weekend dates, snake-danced through the town when Michigan's football team won a victory, and attended concerts by herself when she needed solitude. She found time to earn money by taking pictures of campus clubs and organizations. The editor of the college yearbook asked her to do some photographs. She could be seen, camera in hand, scrambling over buildings or standing on an open balcony. Peg White, as they called her on campus, was the girl who takes pictures. One friend called her a "demon photographer" and predicted "future fame." And though only a sophomore, she was asked to become photo editor of the yearbook. She turned it down because by then her mind was on other matters.

She had been on her way to lunch one day at the campus cafeteria when a young man, on his way out of the

Everett Chapman (Chappie), Margaret's first husband, as a student at Michigan University, 1924

building, trapped Margaret in the revolving door. He kept it spinning until she agreed to go out with him. Everett "Chappie" Chapman, a tall, cheerful, bright young man, was working for his doctorate in electrical engineering. He and Peg fell deeply in love. A professor in the College of Engineering offered them his home for the marriage ceremony. And Margaret, eager to be dressed in traditional white, borrowed his wife's wedding gown.

AN EYE ON THE WORLD

In a small cottage located off campus, Margaret set up housekeeping and started a complex life as wife, student, and part-time breadwinner. She felt even more confused in her multiple roles when she followed Chappie to a teaching job at Purdue University in Indiana. At twenty years of age, she was the youngest faculty wife on campus. She tried to assume her responsibilities, but often she was no older than the students she chaperoned or entertained. In classes, where she continued her science studies, she was regarded as a teacher's wife. She had no friends, and when she felt shaken by marital problems, she did not know where to turn.

Chappie, she discovered, was as dedicated to electric welding as her father had been to his inventions. She accepted the single-mindedness in his work, but she had to compete for his affections with his mother. A beautiful but demanding woman, Mrs. Chapman came for long visits and disrupted the household, pushing Margaret and Chappie apart. The problems became severe, and Margaret sought professional advice. But, by the second year, Margaret had to admit to herself that the marriage could not continue. When it finally broke up, she wept in anguish, distraught at the failure and at the loss of someone she loved so deeply. She stayed on in the Midwest, forcing herself each day to her job in the Natural History Museum in Cleveland, Ohio. At night she routinely took courses at Western Reserve College.

The time finally came when Margaret could close away the pain. She knew then that no one would again touch her

THE GIRL WHO TAKES PICTURES

so deeply. She would say later, "I had been through the valley of the shadow. . . . It was as though everything had been packed into those two short years and would never seem so hard again."

Requiring only one more year of college credits to get a degree, she looked for a beautiful campus far from the scenes of her failed marriage. She chose Cornell University in upstate New York and arrived there in September, 1926, just as the first burst of fall foliage draped the countryside in vivid colors. She found the large campus rimmed with Gothic-style ivy-covered buildings, one of which was the library with its tower and clock that rang out the quarter hour. From the campus hilltop she could look down over a valley of well-marked fields and the famous Lake Cayuga.

Beautiful as the campus was, Margaret felt lost among the thousands of students hurrying to class. Still determined to become a biologist, she filled her program with science courses. And, desperately in need of money, she took a job as a waitress in return for her meals. Later on she had a clerical job. But from her first days at Cornell, she wandered around the campus with her camera in her hand. She had already spotted scenes she wanted to record.

Margaret put to use all she had learned about photography over the years. She had a sense of search, almost a mission, to find the scene that appealed to her. She moved around studying angles for good shots, looking for an effective composition. One day, when a heavy snow made the Cornell buildings look especially beautiful, she cut classes to take pictures. She ran around in the snow, leaving a trail of footprints to make the scene more dramatic. At other times she climbed up to the top of the library tower to survey the campus from a height. She took photographs of a dormitory at dawn seen through a mist, of waterfalls, of college buildings framed by tall trees, and of the distant football stadium with lowering clouds in the foreground.

Evenings Margaret hurried down the steeply sloped streets of Ithaca into the town, where she had located a commercial photographer, Henry R. Head. Impressed with the eagerness of the young girl, he rented her the use of his darkroom. There she made sample enlargements, developing her prints in the Clarence H. White tradition, seeking the misty, blurred effect.

She displayed samples of her work on a table she set up in the corridor outside the college dining room. Students and teachers, eager for mementos of their Cornell years, placed orders for her photographs. It thrilled her when they said, "Why, these don't look like photographs at all."

Encouraged by the number of orders, she printed up hundreds of pictures and pulled together a group of students to work as salespeople on a commission basis. The Cornell Co-op agreed to carry the pictures and, to add to her glory, the *Cornell Alumni News* printed a few of her photographs and paid five dollars for each picture used on a cover. Letters came in from Cornell alumni admiring her work and asking whether she intended to become an architectural photographer.

Margaret saw a dazzling new vista open before her. Architectural photography? Was she talented enough? she asked herself. She liked the feel of a camera in her hand, and she had begun to experience the heady excitement of "catching the moment" when a scene hung together. Still, to make the decisive change from science to photography as a way to earn a living, she needed an objective opinion of her work.

During Easter vacation, Margaret, with a portfolio of pictures under her arm, boarded a train to New York City, where she made her way to the offices of a distinguished architectural firm recommended to her. The head of the company, Benjamin Moscowitz, was rushing off to catch a train. But Margaret pursued him to the elevator, talking and showing him her photographs. When he saw Margaret's picture of the Cornell library tower, he said, "Let's go back and look at these." He called in other members of the firm. They all assured Margaret that, based on the work they saw, she had a future in architectural photography.

Encouraged by these words of praise, Margaret took the train back to Cornell. During the long, slow trip, she had many hours in which to think about her future. In the offing was the dazzling possibility of a career in photography. On the other hand, she had received a job offer from the Museum of Natural History in New York.

"DYNAMOS ARE MORE BEAUTIFUL THAN PEARLS"

Confident about her ability, Margaret chose photography as her life work. With her clear, straightforward way of thinking, she knew it involved great responsibility to embark on such an uncertain career, especially when she knew she had to earn money at once to support herself.

She packed her college degree along with her belongings into her trunk and took a train from Ithaca to Buffalo, New York. There she boarded a night boat that sailed along Lake Erie to Cleveland, Ohio, where she had lived briefly after her marriage ended and where her mother and brother had settled. Her sister, Ruth, had taken law courses and was working in Chicago for the American Bar Association.

Margaret's award-winning photograph of a 200-ton ladle used in the making of steel; Otis Steel Company, 1928

To celebrate her new independence, she became Margaret Bourke-White, attaching her middle name Bourke (also her mother's maiden name) to the family name. In Cleveland, Margaret opened the first Bourke-White Studio in 1927. She turned a one-room apartment into her living-and-work space. Each morning she pushed the in-a-door bed out of the way and made the living room into a reception room. She used the kitchen as her darkroom and the breakfast alcove as her printing room. She washed her prints in the bathtub.

With only one suit in her wardrobe, and that a dull gray, Margaret brightened her appearance with accessories. One day she wore the suit with a red hat and red gloves; the next day with blue hat and blue gloves. In high-heeled shoes, she walked miles of pavement, knocking on the doors of architectural firms recommended by Cornell alumni. She won her first commission from a firm of young architects that, like her, had yet to make its mark. The architects had difficulty getting acceptable photographs of a school they had designed. Margaret saw why when she visited the school and found the building surrounded by muddy grounds and littered with gravel and unused lumber. She spent five days viewing the scene in varying light. She arose at sunrise to look at the school in the morning and returned in the evening to see it in the setting sun. One morning, when the sunrise lighted a cloudless sky, she rushed over to the school only to find the grounds strewn with garbage. She ran to a florist, bought handfuls of asters, stuck them in the mud away from the debris, and shot her pictures from a low angle, over the top of the flowers, showing the school framed by flowers and by the sunrise.

Impressed with her ingenuity as well as her skill, the architects bought several of Margaret's photographs at five dollars each and succeeded in getting them published in *Architecture* magazine.

The first burst of publicity made Margaret a busy photographer. She picked up commissions from banks, landscape artists, and architects. Her photographs of stately homes and gardens had a misty, pictorial quality in the Clarence H. White tradition. Dappled light played over gardens and lily ponds, or was seen through grillwork and leaded glass windows. Her compositions were so effective that *House and Garden*, as well as other magazines, began to feature her work.

Though Margaret was busy with these commissions that paid her expenses, she began to find increasing excitement in an entirely different landscape. Several times a week she drove an old battered car she had bought over to the low-lying industrial valley in downtown Cleveland, called the Flats. Only people who worked there traveled to that bleak stretch of land spread out along the winding Cuyahoga River. But Margaret saw the drama and beauty of modern industry in the Flats. The heavy smoke pouring from the chimneys of the steel mills, the mounds of iron ore, and the roaring freight and automobile traffic fascinated her the way rare jewels might fascinate others. She found form and pattern in smokestacks, in vaulting arches holding up bridges, in tall electric towers, and in cranes. She studied

the tangled scenes at different hours of the day to see them under varying conditions of light; she climbed up on derricks and scaffolds to see them from different angles. When she thought she could isolate a scene that would reveal the power of industry, she set up her tripod and camera, put her head under the cloth, and shot her pictures.

Afterward, in frustration, she threw most of her negatives in the wastepaper basket. She did not know how to capture on film the energy and vital force of this industrial backyard. Accidentally, however, she learned an important lesson. One day, while photographing at the Flats, she saw in her camera a small, dilapidated boat appear on the Cuyahoga inlet framed by the steel mill and tall smokestacks. At each end of the boat stood a man with a pole in his hand, slowly moving the boat along. She quickly shot pictures. When the boat moved out of camera range, she ran down to the banks of the river, explained to the men what she was doing, and implored them to continue moving the boat back and forth for another hour.

That evening, when she developed her prints, she shouted in joy. "That's how my ship came in," she would say in later years. "Here was contrast. In form. In line. In bulk and lighting and balance. The old and the new." That experience taught her the value of contrast for a good photograph or for any work of art. By showing in one frame an ancient way of handling a boat and complex steel structures, she highlighted the modern world of industry.

An early landscape picture—the William H. Albers home; Cincinnati, Ohio, 1929

"DYNAMOS ARE MORE BEAUTIFUL THAN PEARLS"

She carefully placed the pictures in her portfolio and the next day hastened over to an important business executive who was holding up an advertising catalogue until he found the right illustrations. He bought four of Margaret's photographs and paid her more than she had ever earned.

Margaret's fascination with machines and industry seemed a natural extension of her childhood experiences. Still, hers was not a lone voice, for many artists of that time had begun to celebrate American technology.

In the 1920s, artists had a new vision of the United States as a great industrial power that would expand forever and remain a creative force. They found surging drama in steel and electricity, in bridges spanning rivers, in skyscrapers built into the sky. The machines of industry were worshipped as if they were deities. Common, everyday articles like furniture, pots and pans, and dishes became objects of novel design and fashion. And a galaxy of new ideas and terminology soon flashed upon the art world: Machine Esthetic, Machine Age, Industrial Design, Modernism. This was only one aspect of the decade that became known as the "roaring twenties" with its booming economy, its lavish Art Deco design, its jazz, and its gay dances—the fox trot, the shimmy, and the Charleston.

Margaret found beauty and excitement not only in the outward forms of machines but in machines in motion, in action and change, and in the raw process of production. She wanted to see the actual workings of a steel mill. During the many hours she had trudged through the slag and smoke of the Cleveland Flats, she had her eye on the Otis Steel Company, wondering how she could get inside the heavy door marked *Private.* A business acquaintance helped her gain an interview.

She stood before Elroy J. Kulas, president of the company, pleading for permission to take pictures of the making of steel. She spoke about the power she saw in industry and how it reflected the age in which we live. "Steel mills," she said in her earnest, sincere manner, "are at the very heart of industry with the most drama, the most beauty."

Mr. Kulas found Margaret convincing. Still, he hesitated. No one had ever photographed the making of steel. Visitors had been known to pass out from the smoke and heat. Finally he expressed his worry that Margaret might faint from the fumes in the mill.

"I am not the fainting kind," she assured Mr. Kulas.

Persuaded by her self-confidence, he called in other company officials and notified them of Margaret's project. Then he sailed off for a five-month trip to Europe.

Margaret would never forget her first view of the inside of a steel mill. Spread out before her were meaningless shapes, like scenes from abstract paintings. Only after many visits could she adjust to the roar and glare of the mill and put into context the giant hoods and cranes, the huge furnaces, and the sweating workers in heatproof masks and clothes moving about in the dark depths. When the furnaces were pulled, Margaret saw flames spew out of the darkness. Automatic ladles dipped into seething liquid and poured it into molds. Up on the catwalk surveying the flaming mass below, Margaret began to shoot pictures. Or she climbed into an overhead crane and shot down into the molten mass. Sometimes she took pictures from hanging ladders. When

"DYNAMOS ARE MORE BEAUTIFUL THAN PEARLS"

she developed her negatives, she did not recognize anything she had photographed.

Margaret was in trouble. Without realizing it, she had undertaken a colossal project. Technically she could not cope with the problems—with the lack of lighting, with the scorching heat that blistered the varnish off her camera, and with the extreme contrasts in light and shade. Photography had not yet progressed to the use of flashbulbs, film, and lenses adequate to meet the needs of her difficult project.

Plant workers and officials, who expected Margaret to show up for a few days, take her pictures and leave, were astonished to see her return week after week with her heavy 5 × 7 camera and tripod. They worried that she would break a leg or fall into the molten metal. But she stalked the mill, a strange and lonely figure, a woman in a man's workplace, searching for the exact spot and for the light that would enable her to print on film the burst of flame and sparks of the making of steel.

Completely at a loss, she called on Alfred Bemis, a commercial photographer in Cleveland who had helped her out before. "Beme" and his assistant, Earl Leiter, joined Margaret at the steel mill. The three of them experimented with new cameras. They brought in floodlights and laid cables in an effort to get adequate lighting. They shot off flashpans. But nothing worked. Margaret would not give up; the steel mill became the laboratory in which she experimented and learned the basic lessons on how to light a picture. She tried every new device that came into Bemis's store. One day, a photography salesman, on his way to Hollywood to show the film industry new magnesium flares, dropped into the shop. Persuaded to join Bemis, Leiter, and Margaret at the steel mill, he worked out strategy with them as if they were attacking an enemy target. While they waited for the molten metal to reach its "heat" before the pouring, Margaret crawled along the catwalk, preparing angles for her shots. Finally, she set her camera on the crossrail. Then, just as the metal bubbled in the ladles, the magnesium flares were fired off in a cloud of smoke, lighting the scene, and Margaret shot her pictures.

That night, with her friends surrounding her, Margaret developed her negatives. They saw on film great ladles, hooks and cranes, and the actual path of sparks. She had photographed the making of steel.

When Elroy Kulas returned from Europe, Margaret brought him twelve photographs out of about five hundred she had shot. Astonished with what he saw, Kulas bought eight pictures at a hundred dollars each and ordered eight more. He put them in a book called *The Story of Steel*, which he sent to stockholders. The pictures were reproduced in magazines and newspapers.

With her pictures of steel, Margaret was launched on her career. "I feel as if the world has been opened up and I hold all the keys," she wrote to her mother. Other industrialists commissioned her to photograph their plants. She took pictures of ore boats, coal rigs, bridge construction, cylinders, and dynamos. She had an extraordinary eye for design; she could isolate a piece of machinery and show not only its power but its beauty.

To meet the rush of work, she moved from her cramped quarters to a studio high up in the Terminal Tower, Cleve-

The Flats—railroad yard and Terminal Tower in the background; Cleveland, Ohio, 1929

land's tallest skyscraper. A secretary and a technician helped her turn out her work.

At age twenty-four she had become the "girl wonder" of photography. The press rated her "a leader among industrial camera artists of America." Her signature on a photograph became a mark of distinction. Not only was she known as a unique photographer but as a person who disregarded danger in her search for the exact spot for her pictures.

She paid careful attention to her clothes and liked to look fashionable. In the smart look of the day, she wore her dark hair with a dip over one eye.

To a newspaper reporter who found it unusual that a young, attractive woman like Margaret preferred to photograph seamy industrial subjects rather than gardens and ba-

Margaret on location in Cleveland, Ohio, photographed by Ralph Steiner, 1928

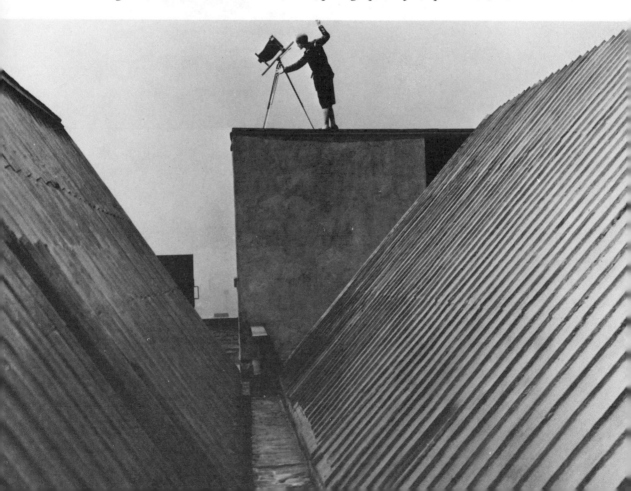

Margaret, a leading industrial photographer at 24

bies, she said, "I dislike bothering with obvious prettiness
... what makes my job as a photographer fascinating is to
hunt and hunt for just the viewpoint that would make
cranes, smokestacks or drawbridges beautiful." In her passion for the industrial scene, she became an ardent exponent
of the Machine Esthetic. "Dynamos are more beautiful than
pearls," she told another interviewer. "The purpose of art,"
she would say, "is to find beauty in the big things of the age.
Today that big thing is industry."

Her reputation spread to the East Coast where Henry
R. Luce, the successful publisher of *Time* magazine, was
working on plans for a new periodical. In the spring of 1929,
Luce sent Margaret a telegram: HAVE JUST SEEN YOUR
STEEL PHOTOGRAPHS. CAN YOU COME TO NEW YORK
WITHIN WEEK AT OUR EXPENSE? Unfamiliar with Luce's
name, Margaret decided to take advantage of the invitation
in order to visit New York. But when she met Luce and listened to his plans, she knew she could not turn down his offer.

WITH A CAMERA IN HER HAND

 At twenty-five years of age, Margaret found a new showcase for her talents that would make her internationally prominent. She accepted Henry Luce's offer of a position as staff photographer and assistant editor on his new magazine. *Fortune,* as it would be called, would explore every aspect of the industrial process from the "steam shovel to the Board of Directors." The camera would be put to new use, to interpret and document the modern world.

Margaret saw at once that Luce's ideas were stretching the concept of photography to a new dimension and that photography itself would have to grow to meet the demands made on it.

Margaret sloshing through the mud on location; Russia, 1930

Filled with excitement at her new position, she phoned an old friend, Ralph Steiner, whom she had met years before at the Clarence H. White School of Photography. Over the years she had seen him from time to time and, admiring him as an honest craftsman, she accepted his critical comments. Early on he had directed her away from trying to make photographs look like paintings, in the Clarence H. White tradition. When he had passed through Cleveland in the late 1920s and visited Margaret, he had ridiculed her fussy need to match the color of her camera cloth to the color of her suit. At that time Margaret had found it fashionable to use a purple cloth when she wore a purple suit, a blue cloth with her blue suit. "What difference does it make what color cloth you focus your pictures with as long as they are good pictures?" he wanted to know. And now in New York to see Henry Luce, Margaret looked up Steiner to show him her latest work. She would never win his admiration, she sorrowfully concluded, and wrote as much in a letter to her mother in May, 1929. "I spent last evening with Steiner, going over my pictures. He is always very critical, you know, and never praises me, but he did say that he thought I had improved, and that my viewpoint was becoming more direct and mature."

For the first couple of years that Margaret worked for *Fortune* magazine, she maintained her studio in Cleveland and traveled from there to her assignments. She gave Luce permission to use her steel photographs as promotional material.

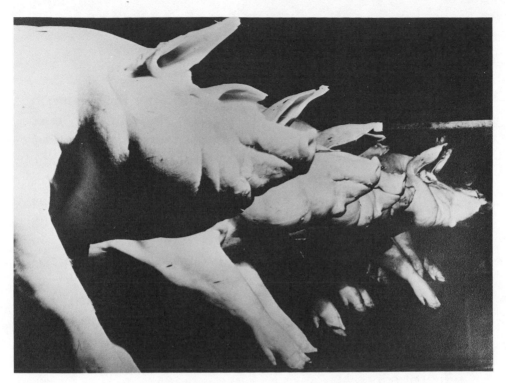

From "Hogs," lead article in Fortune, 1929

One assignment took Margaret to the stockyards of Chicago. Accompanied by Luce's editor Parker Lloyd-Smith, she was to do the photographs for a story on the Swift meat-packing industry. She prowled the plant, trying to figure out how to communicate the force of the billion dollar industry in which over 15 million hogs poured through the yards in a single year and ended up as processed meat. Working closely with Lloyd-Smith, she made a sequence of pictures that together told a story.

She turned her lens on thousands of pigs pouring into the stockyards. She showed how they were prodded into narrow alleys while men stood by appraising their value in dollars and cents. She shot pictures in the slaughterhouse where hogs were reduced to dressed carcasses hanging by the thousands in row upon row from hooks on beams. She showed white-gowned men with flashing, gleaming knives carving the carcasses into different cuts of meat. Then she explored the curing room where thousands of hams hung from rafters. In the final shots, her camera zoomed in on mammoth heaps of pig dust, the ground-up remains of carcasses that would be used as meal for other animals. Writer Lloyd-Smith retched from the putrid odors and fled. But Margaret stayed on in that foul-smelling room getting her photographs. When she left, she quickly ripped the cloth and cables from her cameras because they had absorbed the pungent odors.

"Hogs" became the lead story in the first issue of *Fortune* magazine when it hit the newsstands in February, 1930. In that issue there were three other series of Margaret's pictures. In addition to "Hogs," she told the story of glass from its origin as crumbled fragments of rock to its transformation by the glass blower to beautiful and practical objects. "Trade Routes across the Great Lakes" was an essay on iron, steel, coal, and the freighters that carry raw products to the steel mill. Her final photographs dealt with orchids from their planting to their bloom.

Seventeen series of her photographs appeared during the first year in *Fortune*. If *Fortune* provided her with a showcase for her talents, she gave *Fortune* its style and tone. She did much more. She opened up the field of photography to limitless possibilities when she introduced the concept of telling a story with her photographs. By concentrating on a single subject, she added mood and tension to the series of pictures. She also selected what was significant and made important graphic statements that were often as revealing as the written story. Other photographers and writers were moving in the same direction. But Margaret was one of the pioneers; her work would lead the way to photojournalism and the photo essay, which would become a dominant development in the world of photography.

Many of her industrial photographs are now seen as works of art as well as valuable documents of the industrial process. With an artist's eye, she portrayed the rhythm and pattern in a piece of machinery. Or she isolated the simple beauty in a coil of wire. Or she crowded a frame with detail so rich and telling that it looked like a Renaissance painting. She shot pictures from every angle. Looking from the bottom up, she showed the angular lines of an electric tower. Looking down, she photographed a worker pouring hot liquid into molds.

Margaret arrived at assignments steeped in technical information on the subject so that she could talk knowledgeably to the engineers and plant foremen who guided her through the labyrinth of industrial plants. A bevy of assistants carried her bulky cameras and film packs and set up the lighting.

With her camera in her hand, she never thought about danger. No assignment was too perilous, and her daring exploits became as famous as her photographs. *Dizzy Heights Have No Terror for This Girl Photographer* headlined one newspaper article.

WITH A CAMERA IN HER HAND

For a *Fortune* assignment, she photographed the day-to-day construction of the Chrysler Building, scheduled to become New York's tallest skyscraper. At street level she shot pictures of steel girders spearing space with geometric patterns. She showed the outside and the inside of the hoist that carried men and materials to high floors. She herself rode the hoist to the top level of the skeletal skyscraper. Eight hundred feet above the ground, she clung to a girder and, with an icy wind buffeting her, photographed the massive finial, the upper extremity, of the Chrysler tower before it was sheathed in steel.

"I am not frightened," she shouted to a group of workers who wanted to tie her down to a beam for safety. "I like the feeling of being free," she said.

At the upper level, she watched workers building steel gargoyles out over the streets below. The view from the high floor fascinated her. She became absorbed in the vast urban landscape that stretched for miles south to the tip of the city and from river to river. She looked up into a broad sweep of cloud-filled sky. And she was determined to move her studio from Cleveland to the Chrysler Building.

Margaret rented space for the Bourke-White Studio on the sixty-first floor of the Chrysler Building. Decorator John Vassos designed and furnished the new offices in the modern Art Deco style with built-in furniture made of natural woods, glass, and aluminum. Into one wall, Margaret had an aquarium built for her tropical fish. When she gave

The vitality of industry; the Chrysler Corporation

AN EYE ON THE WORLD

parties, guests shared the huge terraces with praying mantes, tortoises, and two pet alligators a friend had sent from Florida.

Ambitious and energetic, Margaret searched for new worlds to explore, new doors to pry open. From her talk with industrialists in the United States, she became increasingly curious about the Union of Soviet Socialist Republics (until the Revolution of 1917 known as Russia). She had heard that in that land halfway across the world, machines were transforming a backward feudal country into a modern industrial state.

When *Fortune* sent Margaret on assignment to Germany, she decided to push on from there to the country she had heard so much about. *Fortune*, convinced that the Soviet Union would not permit a photographer the freedom to take pictures, would not sponsor her trip. Still, Margaret was determined to go.

She did not pretend that she understood politics. She had no interest in the subject. It did not matter to her that the Soviet Union was building a new kind of society called socialism and that its concepts were considered incompatible with the political philosophy of Western countries. She knew only that in their first Five-Year Plan they were constructing the world's largest dam, that machines were dramatically changing a vast landscape and helping people advance from ignorance and poverty into the benefits of the industrial age.

During her stay in Germany, Margaret bombarded the Soviet Consulate with visits and phone calls asking for a visa that would permit her to enter the country. She impressed the Russian officials with her portfolio of industrial photographs. Sergei Eisenstein, the noted Russian filmmaker whom Margaret had met in the States, interceded in her behalf. She stood by with a trunkload of canned goods to see her through the Soviet food shortage. Tons of cameras and films were ready to be shipped.

Margaret's determination won for her an extraordinary triumph. She was finally handed a visa, and within a few days of her entry into the Soviet Union, she was made a guest of the government. She was provided with an interpreter and sheaves of paper to ease her way through shortages in travel space and the terrible confusion that existed at every level of government.

For five weeks in the summer of 1930, and in two subsequent visits, Margaret covered thousands of miles. To reach outlying districts she traveled by train and by boat, on camel and on horseback. She pushed her way through muddy roads, forded rivers, used caves for her darkroom, and developed film in hotel bathtubs. She took eight hundred pictures that included farm cooperatives, factories, mills, and quarries. She photographed turbines, cranes, derricks, blast furnaces, and pieces of machinery rising everywhere on empty plains. She turned her camera to record the construction of the massive dam at the Dnieper River. She also experimented with the movie camera and did two short films of her trip.

At the same time that she reported on the Soviet industrial development, she described the terrible famine that gripped the country and made people's lives so difficult.

A worker, called an iron puddler, in a steel mill; Stalingrad, 1930

The cans of food she had brought from Germany, which she had shared, had run out, and for a week she lived on baked beans.

As she worked, Margaret reveled in the magic of her camera, excited over the "blackness and whiteness" of photography that "makes it so suitable for industrial subjects.... It is honest and revealing and clean cut, an astounding means of expression and the best for portraying the power and force of industry," was the way she put it.

AN EYE ON THE WORLD

Machines, for Margaret, were things in themselves. They had form and force and were "rich with the breath of doing." She saw that the Soviet Union used machines as beneficent instruments to change the lives of people. For the first time in many years, she noticed people and the relationship of men and women to machines. "They are transforming the economic life of the country which in turn is transforming them," she wrote. She photographed workers, old and young, skilled and unskilled, learning to use tractors

Children in a nursery at a Russian automobile factory, 1931

and dynamos. She watched women working in heavy industry, operating drill presses, and she realized that new futures were open to them. She learned that many women were studying medicine and engineering.

Her passion for machines made her an ally of the socialist state. In turn, the Russians loved Margaret Bourke-White and called the photographer the "artist of the machine age." They appreciated her ability to endure hardships, take risks, and never complain. They also enjoyed her temperament. One day, as she was being driven to a farm collective, a herd of horses galloped by. "Stop," she called to the driver of the car. She tore after the horses on foot, her camera over her shoulder. Her interpreter ran after her with film holders while the driver followed along in the car with reserves of film. She shot pictures of the horses, at first as "dots on the horizon." Closer up, they became "bodies rushing by her."

Margaret was back home in 1931 when her first book was published. *Eyes on Russia*, illustrated with forty photographs, was a record of her experiences in the Soviet Union. Unanimous praise for the book increased her popularity, and she became a success on the lecture circuit. She brought to crowded halls a firsthand report on the exotic, mysterious country thousands of miles away. The *New York Times Magazine* carried a series of her articles and photographs. In 1933, after the United States and the Soviet Union established diplomatic relations, her two travelogues received wide distribution.

She had become a dashing and glamorous figure. Her energy and her inventive mind made her extraordinarily productive. Advertising agencies hired her to put her skills into commercial photography. Buick cars and Goodyear tires became her largest accounts. But she also did glossy ads for silver, food, and cosmetics, making her clients' products appear more attractive than competitors'. She would say that commercial advertising taught her how to work with color film and light to achieve realistic effects. She could make a rubber tire look like rubber and not like stiff cardboard. Advertising paid extremely well, and Margaret became an affluent woman.

For six months of the year she worked for *Fortune* magazine. The other six months she devoted to advertising. A staff of eight helped her turn out her work.

For a brief period in 1934, Margaret concentrated on doing photomurals, a blown-up photograph or series of photographs that cover a wall. She reached a highlight in her career as an industrial photographer in her mural for the National Broadcasting Company. She called it *Trapping the Magical Waves of Sound*. In the mural she showed, in a sequence of photos, the complex pieces of machinery that control the sending and receiving of sound. The photomural, 160 feet in circumference by 10 feet high, decorated the circular reception room of NBC's office in Radio City, New York, and was viewed by thousands of visitors.

While Margaret lived high up in the clouds, her mind filled with machines and commercial accounts, a different drama filled the streets below.

Fortune magazine had begun publishing just as the New York stock market crash of November, 1929, broke over the world and ushered in the turbulent years of the Great Depression. The new publication, addressing itself to the vitality that remained in industry, climbed to success. But the depression had toppled financial empires, putting millions of people out of work. Unemployment cut across all lines, dragging down workers, the middle class, professionals, and artists. In demonstrations and public meetings held across the country, the unemployed demanded jobs and relief through federal programs. Artists—photographers, painters, writers, and dancers—joined in the outcry and used their talents to awaken public conscience to the painful social and economic conditions.

An assignment from *Fortune* would turn Margaret around and force her to confront the realities of the day.

FACES SHE COULD NOT PASS BY

In a tiny two-seater plane, Margaret Bourke-White was flying over the states of the Midwest from the Dakotas to Texas. *Fortune* had assigned her to photograph the effects of months of drought on the once fertile land. Where tall golden wheat and corn used to grow, Margaret looked down over miles of caked, parched earth and dried-up riverbeds. For months a ruthless sun had beat down from a cloudless sky, withering crops and scorching the earth, turning it to fine sand. From the air and from the ground, she photographed the whirling yellow clouds of duststorms that blew with gale strength, clogging the lungs of children, grown-ups, and animals.

Millions of farm people were at the mercy of the drought. Margaret visited farms and watched children being

From *You Have Seen Their Faces*; Lansdale, Arkansas, *1936*

Caked, parched earth—the drought; South Dakota, 1934

put to bed with towels over their faces to keep out the fine dust that seeped through invisible cracks. She saw the poverty and suffering of families who, with sticks of furniture piled on broken-down cars and wagons, drifted along dust-cracked roads looking for work. "Here were faces engraved with the very paralysis of despair. These were faces I could not pass by," she said.

When she returned to New York, her experiences in the dust bowl (as that area of the country came to be called) turned her dreams to nightmares. One terrifying night she dreamed that an avalanche of cars was careening down on her. She could not escape them. They were about to crush her when she awakened and found herself writhing on the floor with a strained back.

Her dreams reflected her real conflicts over her advertising accounts. Was she succumbing to the pressure of the advertising world and sacrificing her artistic integrity? she asked herself. Did she tell the truth when she enhanced a product to make people buy it? Is that the way she wanted to use her photography? With her good sense and her eye for news, she had begun to realize that the center of excitement had shifted to the streets and to the culture that had grown up around the Great Depression. She took steps to redirect her life, cutting herself loose from the advertising world and turning her fierce capacity for work to the conditions in the United States.

The social upheaval of the 1930s had gripped many talented artists. Margaret, too, wanted to understand the conditions in which people lived and how events affected them. And she wanted to put photography to use to communicate her new social awareness, to document the miserable conditions of poverty-stricken families. Perhaps a book, she thought, would tell the story. But she wanted a collaborator, a writer who would describe what she photographed. Word soon reached her that Erskine Caldwell, the writer, was looking for a photographer.

Caldwell's book and play *Tobacco Road* had made him a successful but controversial figure. Born and raised in the South, he knew firsthand the sordid aspects of southern life he described so poignantly in his work. Now he wanted to write a book and document with photographs the suffering and poverty with which he was familiar. He was especially sensitive to the degrading conditions suffered by black people.

Caldwell's appearance gave no hint of his inner complexity. Tall and broad-shouldered, with sandy-colored hair and light blue eyes, he had a soft, gentle voice. He could be charming and talk at great length on many subjects; or he could use words sparingly. In his somber moods, he froze into silence.

The joint Bourke-White–Caldwell project got under way in June, 1936. Margaret flew down to Georgia and joined Caldwell there. In his small car she stowed five cameras, tripods, flashbulbs, and film. She also securely tucked away two glass jars that contained egg cases of praying mantes. She was in the midst of photographing their dramatic life cycle and would not leave them behind.

During the first few days, each tried to judge the other's character. Long experience with a silent father had taught Margaret how to cope with Caldwell's silence. She kept quiet and carefully gazed out at the southern countryside. Margaret had learned before the project started that Caldwell had reservations about working with a woman, and with Bourke-White in particular whose work he did not admire. A few days into the venture, it looked as if she would have to pack her gear and head for home. Caldwell showed up in her hotel room one evening and explained that he felt like a "tourist guide" because she had nothing to offer. Perhaps they had better call the whole thing off, he thought. Shocked, because the project was so meaningful to her, Margaret burst into tears. The emotional outburst

Margaret, photographing the life cycle of a praying mantis, as photographed by Carl Mydans, 1938

cleared the air. In the following days, they found themselves drawn to each other and then they were in love. Their relationship became idyllic, bringing into blossom each one's more generous nature. And the collaboration was saved.

Caldwell had studied the conditions of the southern tenant farmer and sharecropper. In his soft voice he tutored Margaret with facts and figures, helping her understand the poverty of the farm population. Its crippling effects were visible in every state they covered in the Deep South, from Georgia and South Carolina to Arkansas and Louisiana. She

FACES SHE COULD NOT PASS BY

saw walls of wooden huts lined with newspapers to keep out the cold; children sharing a single coat and pair of shoes— one day one child wore them to school and the next day another; crumbs of food for meals; and faces of men and women lined with deep ruts like dried-up riverbeds. She saw black people suffering the wretched insults of racism.

Typically, Margaret did not romanticize the misery she saw, nor did she recoil before painful realities. Poverty was destructive, and she showed its ravages in the misshapen bodies and diseased faces of the poor.

You Have Seen Their Faces, the joint Bourke-White– Caldwell book, became a landmark publication. In words and photographs their work dramatically documented the miserable conditions among the country's sharecroppers. Margaret's sixty-four pictures are direct, stark, and com- pelling. They represent some of her best work.

Margaret's photographs, as well as those of photogra- phers Dorothea Lange, Arthur Rothstein, Walker Evans, and Ben Shahn, influenced the U.S. government to take ac- tion in behalf of the poor farm population.

Vital areas of activity had opened up to Margaret with her increased social awareness. In 1935 she had written an article called "Dust Changes America" for a liberal weekly, the *Nation*, on her experiences during the drought. That same publication carried another of her articles, in which she suggested that photographers use the medium to portray the real world around them. In 1936 Margaret joined the first American Writers' Congress. At a conference in New York City, a broad coalition of distinguished artists and authors, among them Edward Steichen, Ralph Steiner, Paul Manship, and Norman Bel Geddes, discussed the relationship between art and society. They drew up a program that included the defense of freedom of expression at home and the fight against war and fascism abroad.

Margaret exhibited her work and lectured at the Photo League. This newly formed organization of working photographers was actively engaged in recording and illuminating economic and social conditions. Distinguished artists lectured, taught, or exhibited their work at the League's New York City headquarters. Among them were Paul Strand, Henri Cartier-Bresson, Edward Weston, Lewis Hine, and Dorothea Lange.

Margaret's initiation into the world of political and social activity enlarged her perception of events. She brought her enriched vision to the mainstream of her work. This became apparent when she undertook assignments for a new publication.

Life magazine was still in the planning stage when Bourke-White was asked to join the staff as one of four leading photographers. Its publisher, Henry R. Luce (also the publisher of *Fortune*) envisioned another new kind of publication, a photographic magazine. It would visually communicate the news of the day in a well-planned series of pictures. Photographers would be sent to all parts of the world to record important events and work up background material for their stories.

Life's editors sent Margaret to Fort Peck, Montana, to do a prepublication workup of a dam under construction.

FACES SHE COULD NOT PASS BY

They figured she would turn out brilliant industrial photographs, which they would use as fill-in material in an issue of the magazine.

On the flatlands of northeastern Montana, Margaret found the world's largest earthen dam being built. The government-funded, multimillion-dollar project had put to work ten thousand unemployed men. With the bulky cameras she favored, Margaret moved around the construction site, shooting pictures of massive concrete columns, the underpinnings of the huge dam. She took pictures of construction equipment including a huge steel "liner" with its steel disks and radiating steel prongs. But to her industrial photographs she added something new. She had become curious about the way workers and their families lived, and about the thousands of people drawn like magnets to the shantytowns that had mushroomed around the construction site.

From the air Margaret shot pictures of miles of barren, dusty plains with rows of small wooden shacks hugging the foreground. From the street she focused on the shabby, broken-down homes where families lived with no indoor running water, poor sanitation facilities, and a total lack of health care. She showed the sleazy, rundown shops that lined the one-street towns. She took her cameras indoors, into the dance halls where young women called taxi-dancers worked through the night earning five cents a dance to partner a man. In saloons she showed men and women lining the bars. One of the photographs showed a small, sad-looking child sitting on a saloon bar. Her mother had a job in the saloon, and for want of child care facilities, she had to take

No child care facilities—a little girl on a saloon bar; Fort Peck, Montana, 1936

the little girl to work with her. Margaret recorded the scant, sordid lives led by people cut adrift from established centers of human activity.

Her photographs astonished the editors of *Life*. These emotionally packed pictures about people were not what they had in mind. But they found Margaret's story so revealing that they changed their plans. On the cover of *Life*'s first issue, they put Margaret's photographs of the giant concrete columns of the Fort Peck dam. Two men, looking insignificant at the base of the columns, give them scale. Her other photographs of the construction site became the strong opening photo essay.

Margaret had given the first issue of *Fortune* magazine its lead story in 1930. In 1936, her creative photography and strong story sense helped launch *Life* into orbit. The graphic presentation of the news had dazzling public appeal. *Life*'s publishers could hardly keep up with the first months' huge demand. With the magazine's inordinate success, Margaret became one of the most widely known and internationally popular photographers.

Progress in camera technology made possible the pictorial magazine. New camera equipment, imported from abroad, was light and flexible, easy to handle. A few photographers of that period, using these candid or miniature cameras, could take pictures in a fraction of a second. What the pictures lost in rich detail, they made up in spontaneity and naturalness. With one or two of these cameras dangling around their necks, photographers could push their way into crowded news scenes that were once the exclusive preserve of the writer. A photographer could record a scene more quickly than a reporter could take down words. And photography was universally understood, leaping barriers of language and cultural differences. A new breed of editors learned how to arrange a series of pictures for telling impact.

Picture magazines such as *Life, Look, Peek, Pic,* and others swamped the newsstands. A flood of talent fought its way into the broadening field of news photography. Ruthless competition for jobs set the tone of the marketplace. Those who made it to the top had to be tough, bold, and aggressive. They had to produce exciting, newsworthy pictures to get key assignments. It has been said that *Life* editors pitted their talented photographers against each other to make them turn out innovative work.

In this arena, dominated by men, Margaret Bourke-White became a celebrity. Did being a woman help her or hinder her? she was often asked. Colleagues have mentioned that she used her feminine attractiveness to win entry into high places, that influential men vied with each other to carry her gear. Time, Inc. president Henry Luce was seen lugging around her heavy cameras. He would be followed in later years by generals, admirals, and even a potentate or two. Margaret could be charming, flash a winning smile, and create eddies of excitement around her. And she was often presumptuous, requesting colleagues to transport home cartons of material from foreign assignments. But, above all, she had the self-confidence to carve out her own space and write her own rules. Crucial to her success was not gender, as she had made abundantly clear, but drive, talent, and courage.

"NERVOUS AS A CAT"

"Photography is my life work," Margaret told an interviewer for *Scholastic* magazine in 1937. For young people interested in becoming industrial or news photographers, she had straightforward advice. "You have to be strong and healthy," she said. She went into further detail at a college conference on careers where she said, "You have to be as strong as a horse . . . to work under tension, sleep irregular hours and eat on the run." Essential, also, were "patience, courage, a sense for detail and an honest view of life." A few years later she would add to these qualifications a readiness to work under dangerous conditions such as riding in bomber raids and dangling from helicopters.

Margaret, the internationally successful photographer

But Peggy, or Maggie, as she was called on the job, had other outstanding qualities, according to a *Life* photo editor. She had a wonderful eye, a sense of composition, and above all, "the tenacity and persistence that resulted in pictures that could not be otherwise taken."

She was besieged with requests to lecture, give interviews, attend elegant functions, and support worthwhile causes. In her busy schedule she found time to dance, swim, and ski. Her prematurely white hair made her strikingly beautiful. Natural high color suffused her strong cheekbones. She clothed her slim, willowy figure in imported, couturier-designed clothes, favoring the color red. For work she wore tailored pants suits long before they became the fashion.

Many on her technical staff knew Margaret could be kind and responsive to their needs. Because they saw how mercilessly she drove herself, they endured long hours and hard work. In the darkroom, technicians Oscar Graubner and later George Karas worked to bring her prints up to star quality. Peggy Sargent managed the myriad office and technical details. At social functions, Margaret showed her keen wit and charm. But when she worked, she was a terror.

"For a few minutes I think I could commit murder if anyone gets in the way of what I am doing," she once said. "A picture is perishable. . . . There is that moment when people and surroundings fall into a relationship that is utterly pictorial. The Picture is suddenly there. It could vanish in a minute . . . and forever." While trying to seize that moment, she would get as "nervous as a cat" and, driven by powerful inner pressure, would become blind to every

On location, young men assisting with flash bulbs and lights

danger and risk. She would push everything and everyone out
of her way and go after the picture. Then came the thrill of
putting her face in the camera, pivoting her camera around,
and finding herself locked in with what she saw in the lens.
At such times, she said, "the outside world is closed away as
effectively as if the genie of the lamp had clapped his hands
and dissolved the earth leaving me with my camera and my
subject."

"NERVOUS AS A CAT"

She tried to make "Skinny," as she called Erskine Caldwell, understand her commitment to her work—that she cherished it even above marriage. For "Kit," as Caldwell called her, and Skinny there was only leftover time from their individual careers. Still, they were deeply in love and saw each other whenever possible.

From the mid-1930s on, Margaret traveled over a world in turmoil as one of *Life*'s leading photographers. Free to improvise and to work out the nature of her assignments, she sent back photographs enriched by her own social awareness. Sometimes the only woman photographer present, she pushed and shoved her way into a crowded newsroom as in Washington, D.C., where she covered the second inauguration of President Franklin D. Roosevelt. She flew to Louisville, Ohio, when disastrous floods put three quarters of the city under water. She hitchhiked from the airport, thumbing rides in rowboats. Threats were made to her life and cameras when she photographed a story of corruption in Jersey City under boss Mayor Hague. Then in 1937 she was sent to cover the appointment of a new governor-general of Canada.

Margaret packed her camera gear, warm clothes, and a ski suit she would live and work in for days. In her luggage she carefully stowed her butterflies. Determined to photograph their life cycle, she had raised them from eggs to caterpillars to the chrysalis stage, and now they were about to hatch.

She flew to the Canadian Northwest where a small pontoon plane picked her up and flew her along the isolated waterways to join the touring Canadian governor-general,

Butterflies ready to hatch; the Arctic, 1937

Lord Tweedsmuir, and his party. They explored the barren lands of the Arctic on an old-fashioned wood-burning steamboat, the S.S. *Distributor*. Margaret shot pictures of the Arctic tundra, those vast empty treeless plains covered by ice, as well as pictures of the sparse trapper camps and communities where Canadian Eskimos had learned from their ancestors how to work and live in the frozen north.

Aboard ship, Margaret's butterflies had become the important topic of conversation. "Hey, Maggie, when is the

"NERVOUS AS A CAT"

"Koptanna and her baby Nalsuyals;" the Arctic, 1937

blessed event coming?" Lord Tweedsmuir wanted to know.
Margaret had taped ten wriggling chrysalises to the rail of
the ship. As in childhood, she kept a round-the-clock vigil.
The governor-general gave her books to read, and others
brought her food. Then, just as the ship reached the middle
of Great Bear Lake, far up north in the Arctic Circle, the
chrysalises split open. The captain, true to his word,
brought the ship to a halt so that its vibrations would not
disturb the delicate photographs. Lord Tweedsmuir and an
aide-de-camp handed Margaret film packs. Twenty minutes

AN EYE ON THE WORLD

later, ten mourning cloak butterflies had begun to push their way out of the chrysalises. "For thirty years," said the captain, "I've sailed this ship, and I never stopped it even if a man fell overboard, and here I stop it for a damn butterfly." Margaret fed the newly hatched insects a sweet mixture of sugar and water and let them fly away into the Arctic.

At the small trading posts in the desolate north where the ship stopped for mail and supplies, Margaret found cablegrams from Erskine Caldwell awaiting her. COME HOME . . . he wired.

Margaret had deep feelings for Caldwell, and she wavered. But long before the feminist revolution of the 1960s, she had defined her life in terms of her work. She had freed herself from the traditional roles—marriage and family—by which women then shaped their lives. She had become independent, self-sufficient, and filled with the pride of accomplishment. Marriage might cut into her independence and trap her into conflicts. Should she go out on an assignment or should she stay at home? Could she have a family and a full career as well? She knew she needed inner peace. That was her secret. Freedom from conflict gave her strength. She could be single-minded in her work and handle the excitement and turmoil of the world in which she moved.

She tried to put Caldwell out of her mind as she went off in search of a small plane for an additional assignment from *Life*. The editors wanted a photo story on how the Arctic Ocean looked during the summer. She chartered an old-fashioned vintage plane flown by an expert pilot, Art Rankin. He knew every inch of the unmapped land that lay covered by thick layers of ice ten months of the year. Joining her as fellow passengers on the plane were a bishop on his way to visit remote villages and a composer who wrote travel books.

The small plane flew from a tiny Canadian town toward Cameron Bay, 350 miles further into the Arctic Ocean. The pilot had removed the door of the plane and tied Margaret to the base of the seat so that she could lean out and take pictures. When she hung too far out, the composer tugged at the rope and hauled her back in. She was shooting pictures of the icy patterns below when everything turned gray. A fog had rolled in, completely blocking visibility. The pilot, navigating through the turbulent sky and worried he would run out of fuel, brought the plane down on a spit of land attached to a rocky cliff. Margaret and her three companions found themselves marooned on an uninhabited island in the barren Lewes River. The plane radio, too weak to transmit messages to the nearest inhabited island, 300 miles away, could only receive messages. "Art Rankin's plane unreported," they heard over the radio. And then an additional message was broadcast: "Margaret Bourke-White, Skinny wants to know when are you coming home?"

The four marooned people stretched their emergency rations and kept their spirits up by singing, talking, and drinking tea brewed over odd pieces of kindling. At the end of the second day, a sliver of light broke through the fog. The pilot rushed everyone into the plane and flew through the strand of visibility, only to find himself buffeted by a driving storm. Two hours later, he landed the plane at a small settlement. Margaret sent Caldwell a message that she was returning.

For the balance of that year, 1937, Margaret worked in the United States doing masterful photographs of Hollywood and of the Mt. Wilson Observatory, among others. In early 1938, *Life* sent her abroad to do a photo story on Czechoslovakia. Accompanied by Erskine Caldwell, she spent six months in Europe working on *Life* assignments, as well as on another joint book with Caldwell.

By 1938, Europe was trembling before the savage onslaught of German Nazi aggression. Hitler's armies had already annexed Austria. Refugees from that country had fled to Czechoslovakia for safety, and their lives were again in danger when the Germans threatened to annex the German-speaking territory along the Czech border called the Sudetenland.

Bourke-White recorded for *Life* the terror of people trapped by Nazi violence and racial hatred. By March, 1939, when the Bourke-White–Caldwell book *North of the Danube* was published, Hitler had already annexed all of Czechoslovakia and the world was forewarned of its terrible fate— World War II.

Returning from Europe with Caldwell aboard the S.S. *Aquitania*, Margaret made the decision to try marriage once more. To avoid the publicity that would attend the marriage of two well-known people whose romance was public knowledge, she and Caldwell decided to fly from New York to Nevada. In Reno they rented a taxi to take them to a deserted town called Silver City, where they found a pastor who agreed to marry them in an old unused church. The taxi driver and a shopkeeper were witnesses.

Returning East, Margaret and Caldwell found a house in Darien, Connecticut. On a dead-end road in a wooded, hilly section of the countryside, they furnished a large colonial home, setting aside a studio for Caldwell and work space for Margaret. He would write short stories and novels. She would record in photographs the life histories of insects. That was their plan in April, 1939. A year later Margaret took a leave of absence from *Life* magazine and put in a few months as chief photographer for *P.M.*, a new daily newspaper. Margaret knew *P.M.*'s creator, Ralph Ingersoll, from his days as her editor on *Fortune* and later as vice-president and general manager of Time, Inc., the parent organization of both *Fortune* and *Life*. Ingersoll hoped to put together a crusading liberal newspaper. To make sure its editorial policy was not influenced by big business, the newspaper would not carry advertising.

During the period that Margaret worked for *P.M.*, she and Caldwell pooled their talents again. Traveling over ten thousand miles of the United States, they recorded in words and pictures the everyday life of rural and city people. By the time their book *Say, Is This the U.S.A.?* was published in 1941, World War II had unleashed its full terror in Europe and Asia. Margaret Bourke-White made the decision to return to the staff of *Life* and accepted assignments that would take her to the focal points of the world's turmoil.

Margaret and husband Erskine Caldwell, Christmas card, 1940

"NERVOUS AS A CAT"

"DOING ALL THE THINGS THAT WOMEN NEVER DO"

Margaret stood on the balcony of her room at the National Hotel in Moscow and looked out over the heart of the city. Spread out before her was Red Square, and across the square she could see the Kremlin, the Russian seat of government, with its ancient buildings and churches surrounded by a wall. Outside the Kremlin wall stood St. Basil's Cathedral, its golden domes and towers decorating the sky.

She and Erskine had arrived in the Soviet Union toward the end of May, 1941. To be sure they would get to Moscow safely, they avoided war-torn Europe and took the Western route. They flew across the Pacific Ocean, with stops in China where Margaret took portraits of Chinese

Lifeboat survivors, en route to North African war front, waving to a British Airforce search plane, 1942

85

leaders. From China they flew to Moscow. Within a few days of their arrival, they were given permission to travel through the south of the Soviet Union where Margaret would take pictures. On their way to the Black Sea, stopping at farm collectives and rest homes, they could feel the growing tension in the air. Crowds of people were pressed together around communal radios and loudspeakers in public squares listening to announcements. On June 22, they heard the news—the Germans had dropped bombs on Soviet cities along the southern border. Russian troops were being rushed into battle.

Her *Life* editors had foreseen that World War II might spread to the Soviet Union. They sent Margaret there relying on her popularity with government officials from her visits ten years before. And now, as the German attack on the Soviet Union began, she was the only accredited U.S. photographer there.

In her hotel room in Moscow, she had stashed away the six hundred pounds of camera equipment she had brought with her. There were three thousand flashbulbs, film packs, five cameras, twenty-two lenses, tanks, developer, tools for repairing equipment, and replacements for parts. She was ready to shoot pictures of the war when the military, to protect troop actions from spies, issued orders during the first few days that anyone caught with a camera would be arrested and jailed. For three weeks she beseeched officials to relent, to let her shoot her pictures that, she convinced them, could favorably influence public opinion in the United States. She finally won a photographer's "passport," only to be advised by the U.S. ambassador that all U.S. citizens were being immediately evacuated.

Margaret and Erskine refused to leave Moscow.

They took long walks through the freezing city. Rain and snow pelted Moscow and the countryside, the worst spring weather in anyone's memory. Everywhere they saw people prepare for war. Young children were removed to the countryside; truckloads of men filed through Red Square on the way to the front; women, older men, and older children served as fireguards and helped enforce blackout rules; the golden domes of St. Basil's and the Kremlin palaces were painted a dull gray; and shelters were dug deep into the earth. Bourke-White and Caldwell were in a subway shelter on July 22 when the first German bombs fell on Moscow.

The next day they hurried over to Spazzo House, the temporary headquarters of the U.S. Embassy in Moscow. From the rooftop of Spazzo House or from the open balcony outside her hotel rooms, Margaret would stand at night and record the unearthly spectacle of the German bombardment of Moscow. By the light from flaming incendiary bombs she shot her pictures. In her camera she tracked parachute flares dropping to earth, bombs bursting over targets, and Russian searchlights piercing the sky pinning down German planes for their antiaircraft guns.

While bombers whizzed overhead, she and Caldwell took turns slipping through blacked-out streets to the radio station where they broadcast "live" to U.S. audiences their reports on the attack and defense of Moscow.

"DOING ALL THE THINGS THAT WOMEN NEVER DO"

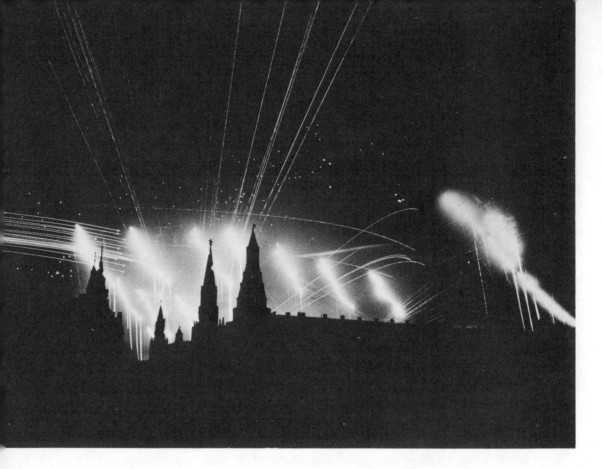

The night bombing of the Kremlin; Moscow, July, 1941

Margaret scored a journalistic scoop with her exclusive photos. She capped that with an unprecedented private photo session with Russia's wartime leader, Josef Stalin. Guards led her through winding corridors into the depths of the Kremlin. Ushered into Stalin's inner office, she saw before her a dour, granite-faced man. In her nervousness over the interview, she dropped flashbulbs all over the floor. She was down on her knees scrambling after them when she looked up and saw Stalin laughing at her. She photographed him with a rare smile on his face. *Life* featured this unusual por-

AN EYE ON THE WORLD

In Russian fur hats, returning home by convoy through the Arctic, 1941

trait of Stalin, as well as Margaret's account of how she made him smile.

In the fall of 1941, Bourke-White and Caldwell were taken, along with other foreign journalists, to Smolensk, the Russian war front. They sloshed through miles of bombed-out countryside, flattening themselves in mud-filled fields when German bombers flew overhead. As the Russians retreated before the German onslaught, Margaret saw them put into effect their "scorched earth" policy. They burned everything in the path of the enemy that they could not cart away—homes, barns, electrical installations. Factories were dismantled and, with the workers and their families, removed to remote sites. The great dam at the Dnieper River, which Margaret had seen the Russians build ten years before, was blown up.

More than ever, with a camera in her hand and pressured by *Life* to send more of her exclusive pictures, Margaret became blind to danger and death. She broke every rule for safety. In Moscow she hid under the bed in her hotel rooms to elude blackout wardens rushing everyone into shelters; or she sneaked out to the open balcony or onto the rooftop as bombs fell. She missed by one second the bomb that fell on Spazzo House. That time, when she heard the telltale whizz overhead, she scrambled down from the roof into the house and flattened herself on the floor. The windows crashed in around her, cutting her fingers, but she escaped a heavy ventilator blown in from the windowsill. She drove herself so mercilessly that she began to feel like a different person, unreal, emptied of feelings—"strange, remote, immune," she would say. She shot pictures of the horrors of war—mass destruction and the innocent dead huddled in doorways. "War is war," she said, "and it has to be recorded."

At a later date she would describe more fully how she felt. "It is as though a protecting screen draws itself across my mind and makes it possible to consider . . . the technique of photography . . . as though I were making an abstract composition. This blind lasts as long as it is needed . . . while I am actually operating the camera. Days later, when I develop the negatives, I [am] surprised to find I cannot bring myself to look at the films. I have to have someone else handle and sort them for me."

Bourke-White and Caldwell returned to the United States in the late fall aboard a cargo ship, part of a convoy, that made its way over the Arctic Ocean and the North Sea. They arrived home in time to fulfill lecture engagements. People everywhere wanted to hear Margaret's eyewitness account of the German invasion of the Soviet Union and the Soviet counterattacks. She spent time in her Connecticut home to write the book *Shooting the Russian War*.

In December, 1941, the United States entered World War II. And Bourke-White, with few to equal her in courage and skill, became the first woman photographer accredited to the U.S. Air Force. She was stationed in England, where U.S. bombers were preparing their attack on the Continent. During short trips into London, she did a portrait of Winston Churchill, the English prime minister and head of the war effort, that *Life* featured on a cover.

In England, Margaret learned of Allied plans to open another war front in North Africa. Determined to be at the center of action, she had herself transferred to Africa and was assigned passage on a transport carrying troops, including women in the armed forces called WACS (Women's Army Corps), as well as medical personnel.

The night before the ship was scheduled to reach its destination, it was torpedoed by a German submarine. Margaret, dumped out of her bunk by the jolt, quickly dressed, grabbed a small knapsack in which she kept a camera and film, and fought her way through corridors and up the stairs. While thousands were filing to their lifeboat stations,

Margaret stood on the deck shooting photographs. Only when she heard "Abandon ship!" did she rush to her assigned place and step into a lifeboat. The lifeboat was half flooded and had a broken rudder, but Margaret, along with the other passengers, used their helmets to scoop out the water. When she could, she helped row the boat. Never had Margaret been so touched by an experience. Warmth and understanding for people surged through her as she watched these men and women draw on deep inner strength in the face of catastrophe. They showed concern for one another and handled their fears by telling jokes, laughing, and singing. After twenty hours of barely keeping afloat on a rough sea, a navy destroyer picked them up. Margaret had seen other lifeboats vanish from view.

For six months Margaret remained in Algeria, where the survivors were taken. During that time she became the only woman to fly in a bombing raid. To ensure her safety, she went through rigorous drilling in rules and regulations governing such missions. Her bomber and thirty-two others, called Flying Fortresses, flew over an airfield near Tunis and dropped their bombs on German troops and planes, blasting them off the field. The successful raid helped to make the African front an Allied stronghold.

From Africa, Margaret returned to the United States. Her marriage to Caldwell had already broken up. She admitted she was unable to compromise with her work. "Mine is a life into which marriage does not fit very well," she said.

She again returned to the war front, this time to Italy. In recognition of her skill in industrial and engineering photography, the U.S. Department of Defense requested

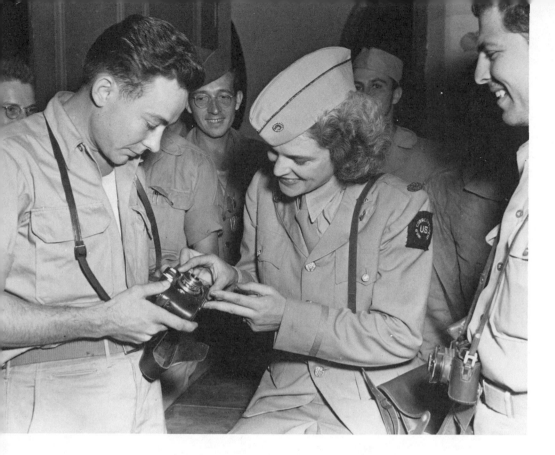

With two army photographers; North Africa, 1943

that she make a photographic record of the Services of Supply. This little-known branch of the army managed the transportation of supplies to the front. Margaret's photos would bring recognition to the vital work of the Engineers, Signal, and Medical Corps.

In Italy, Margaret found her way into the Cassino Valley, where one of the grimmest battles of the war was taking place. U.S. forces were trying to dislodge the enemy entrenched in surrounding hills. For five months Margaret stayed with the Allied forces, covering the heavy fighting on the ground and in the air. She flew in a light plane called a

"DOING ALL THE THINGS THAT WOMEN NEVER DO"

Piper Cub on its dangerous missions to spot enemy positions. On one flight, she was busy taking pictures of the shell-pocked earth beneath her and did not notice four German fighter planes in pursuit. Only the extreme skill of the American pilot, who quickly took a steep dive and flew the plane beneath treetops and over a streambed, brought the Cub safely back to base.

As World War II came to a close in the bitter spring of 1945, Margaret Bourke-White entered Germany with the victorious U.S. armies under General George C. Patton. In the war's aftermath, she saw the burned-out cities. Far

A survivor of the Holocaust; Leipzig-Mochau concentration camp; Germany, 1945

worse, she bore witness to the human wreckage that resulted from the Nazi policy of political repression and genocide
against the Jews. In concentration camps, where millions
had been put to death, she found hollow-eyed survivors.
Outside the camps were fields piled high with human bones.
How could she take photographs of such atrocities? She was
in a stupor, she said, as if she had a veil over her mind. "Cor-
respondents," she explained, "are in a privileged and sometimes unhappy position. . . . They have an obligation to pass
on what they see to others." Her awesome photographs of
the Holocaust, as we now call the German atrocities,
stunned the world. They have become permanent documents of that period.

"EYES LIKE THE EAGLE"

"Do you know how to spin?" Margaret was asked when she arrived in India in the spring of 1946.

"Oh, I didn't come to spin. . . . I came to photograph the Mahatma spinning," she replied.

"How can you understand the Mahatma unless you know how to spin?" came the question.

Margaret persisted, but no amount of charm and persuasion would get her past secretaries and aides to photograph Mahatma Gandhi of India unless she learned how to use the charkha, the spinning wheel. It had become the symbol of the nonviolent struggle for India's independence from England.

Margaret, an aerial photographer, dangling by cable from a whirlybird, 1951

Gandhi's granddaughter taught Margaret how to spin. She showed her how to sit on the floor with her legs crossed before her in front of the old-fashioned wooden wheel and work its simple mechanism. Margaret, the photographer of the machine age, was amazed at her clumsiness. She entangled herself in the thread, breaking it, and was unable to spin out a continuous piece of yarn. But she finally learned how to spin. She learned more; she learned how to slow her pace. In India she could not charge around pushing people and things out of her way. Here a monumental struggle was being waged by a different set of rules.

The leader of the struggle, Mohandas K. Gandhi, had been in jail many times for his beliefs. Millions of people loved him and became his devoted followers, calling him *Mahatma*, meaning "Great Soul." He led the people in acts of civil disobedience, such as the refusal to pay taxes and the boycott of all English goods. The Indian people began to produce their own cloth, and the spinning wheel in every home symbolized their strength and independence. With the eyes of the world on him, Gandhi often went into a "fast unto death" to win concessions from England and reforms from the corrupt and powerful Indian princes.

Margaret had read books and articles on India for background material, but only when she was in India did she fully understand the profound nature of the country's many problems. She was subdued and nervous when she was finally ushered into Gandhi's presence. It was Monday, his day of silence. She saw before her a man of seventy-six years of age, gaunt, brown-skinned, wearing spectacles, sitting cross-legged on the floor, his spinning wheel at his side.

AN EYE ON THE WORLD

Mahatma Gandhi on his day of silence; next to him his charka, a simple spinning wheel; India, 1946

Dressed only in a homespun white loincloth, he was deeply immersed in reading piles of newspaper clippings. In order not to shatter the silence in the room, Margaret was permitted to use only three small, or peanut, flashbulbs for lighting. She fumbled with two of them, spoiling them. With the third, she took the now famous photograph of a relaxed, vital Gandhi sitting beside his spinning wheel, reading.

To carry out her *Life* assignment to do an in-depth study of conditions in India, Bourke-White spent most of 1946 there and returned for lengthy visits in 1947 and 1948. She traveled extensively over the country making a record of the lavish, wanton luxury of India's princes and the famine and disease that plagued millions of the poor. In the tanneries in the south, she found young children working in lime pits that corroded their flesh. In Calcutta she took photographs of decaying bodies over which vultures were swooping—scenes from which tough journalists fled.

Independence could only improve conditions, Margaret thought. And when the great day came in 1946 that India won its independence from England and could form its own government, Margaret was there. But with freedom came new chaos. Within India lived two strong and warring religious forces, the Hindus and the Moslems. To accommodate them, and to end their historic violence, India was partitioned into two nations and became Hindu India and Moslem Pakistan. When the actual division of the land took place, Margaret traveled down to the small border villages and there witnessed epic scenes that made her think of the Old Testament. She saw the exodus of millions of people from their ancestral homelands, forced to seek new refuges. They formed an endless line of humanity on the march—men, women, and children, old and young, on foot, in bullock carts, the weak on the backs of the strong. Only in postwar Germany had Margaret beheld such agony and despair. Thousands died from hunger, disease, and the brutal attacks of marauding bands and hostile religious groups.

Despite her observations, Margaret remained hopeful that India would find its way to a more democratic society. Sensitive to the progress of Indian women, she reported that they were entering the educational system and breaking with age-old tradition by removing the veils from their

The dispossessed—a young boy at a refugee camp, near New Delhi; India, 1947

faces. She also learned that the peasants were demanding the breakup of feudal estates and that mill workers were organizing to improve their conditions.

Before her departure from India on January 30, 1948, Margaret paid Gandhi a visit. She had become fond of him, and he of her, though he called her "the torturer" because of her persistence in taking his picture. She spent twenty minutes with Gandhi while he worked on the charkha. She

"EYES LIKE THE EAGLE"

found him less optimistic about peace in the world. Strongly opposed to the manufacture and explosion of the atom bomb, he said he would meet the bomb with prayer and nonviolence rather than with shelters. "I no longer want to live in a world of darkness and madness," he told Margaret.

As she left him, Margaret turned for a last look and wished him good-bye.

A few hours later, Gandhi was struck down by an assassin's bullet while addressing a prayer meeting in New Delhi. Margaret had been the last foreign journalist to see him alive.

Deeply shocked over his death, yet ever the essential photojournalist, she stayed on in India to photograph the funeral procession. She stationed herself on the cornice of a roof and watched the funeral bier pass by. Gandhi's body, covered with rose petals, was on a flag-draped weapons carrier that was on a five-mile course to the shores of the sacred river Jumna. There, in keeping with Hindu tradition, it would be set aflame. A million grieving people formed a mighty procession behind the funeral cortege.

Helped by friends, Margaret was taken along back roads to the site of the funeral pyre. She fought for space on bridges and ramparts, pushing her way through the surging mass of people, shooting pictures. For a few minutes she saw all her work wasted when her camera equipment fell from her hands and packets of film broke open. Someone in the crowd rescued her material. Finally, with only a Rolleiflex around her neck and set in focus, she fought her way through the crowd to a truck and climbed up on the hood. She held her camera up to photograph the moment when the flames of the simple, sandalwood pyre roared upward—and she realized that she was being pushed off the truck. She clung to the windshield, determined to hold on, when two men, the truck's owners, forcibly removed her. She pleaded with them, but nothing worked until voices from the crowd shouted out, "Let the woman stay! . . . she does not stop her work. What a woman! . . . Let her stay." Another woman, clinging to the truck, called to Margaret's persecutors, "She has the agility of a snake, hair like flax, a face like the sun, and eyes like the eagle. You should learn from her zeal." Margaret stayed on the truck and took her pictures.

Gandhi's assassination sent shock waves through the world. *Life* sent other photographers to India to record the funeral procession and the profound grief of the Indian people at the loss of their great apostle of peace. The magazine featured Bourke-White's photographs and those of Cartier-Bresson.

Upon her return to the United States, Margaret stayed in her Connecticut home to complete work on her book about India, *Halfway to Freedom.*

Though at the peak of her career, each assignment was still a challenge. People, and the conditions of their lives, continued to draw Margaret as intensely as machines did when she was younger. Though she had compassion for suffering, her work remained restrained, reflecting objective reality rather than an emotional response. But this restraint cracked when she saw the human suffering during a visit to South Africa in March, 1950.

Margaret knew, as the whole world knew, that apartheid, or apartness, was the legal policy of the South African government to keep black African people separated from white people. It enabled the white minority to stay in power while it deprived the black majority of every human right. Black people in South Africa could not learn to read and write; they could not train for decent jobs or vote or express their opinions. They were barricaded in shantytowns, the victims of police and government brutality.

Margaret rushed through her schedule, taking traditional photographs of government officials, their sports, and social scenes. She shot pictures of the magnificent countryside with its cloudless blue sky. Then, typically, she probed beneath the surface. She made her way, one Sunday, to a gold mine. Gold and diamond mines, worked by black men, formed the backbone of the country's wealth. At this particular compound she found miners putting on a show of traditional dances. It was a way of expressing loneliness for families and villages many had left behind more than a year before to seek livelihood in the mines. Two of the dancers were so beautiful and so graceful that Margaret decided to base her photo essay on them and show where they worked, lived, and slept.

She discovered, on inquiring for their names, that they had no names, only numbers. They worked two miles down a mine shaft in a "remnant" area where cave-ins were frequent. To do a full story, according to Margaret's way of thinking, she had to go down into the mine. Officials were shocked at her suggestion, but she fought them off and showed up at the mine entrance on a prearranged day in warm clothes, a crash helmet on her head, and a whistle around her neck in case of an accident. Attended by reluc-

AN EYE ON THE WORLD

tant mine foremen, she stepped into a mine cage for the slow descent below sea level, into the steamy darkness of the earth. The cage came to rest in a damp, dark pit. A system of air circulation made it possible to breathe.

She found the two miners curled up in a cramped pocket of space, chipping away at rock with pickaxes. She did not recognize them as the dancers of a few nights before. She saw rivers of sweat pouring down their faces and bodies. In their eyes, which would haunt her forever, she saw their deep pain and scarred spirits. In the midst of taking their pictures, she almost fainted from the heat and was relieved to be brought back to the surface of the mine. But she knew that these black men spent most of their lives down in the pit and that many collapsed and died from work and

Gold miners, photographed while working two miles underground; Johannesburg, South Africa, 1950

heat. Margaret, in her photo story, showed the way miners were forced to live in windowless concrete barracks where they slept "rolled up like sausages on the floor."

The photograph of the two black miners became one of Margaret's favorites. She saw the "sorrow of all mankind in the miners' eyes," she would say. She ended the lengthy essay with the picture of a three-year-old black child standing behind barbed wire.

At the mad pace at which she worked, Margaret moved from one daring feat to another. Often she asked for the most dangerous assignment, or she thought one up.

In 1950 she had gone into the bowels of the earth for her South African photographs. A year later she hung suspended by cable from a helicopter high above the United States and its bordering seas to get a view of the country from the top down. She had become *Life*'s aerial photographer. To prepare for this assignment, she had consulted navy helicopter pilots. And for months she barnstormed the country with traffic patrols and pipeline inspectors, flying so low over bridges and mountains that she could almost stretch out her hand and touch them.

She felt perfectly safe hanging from a helicopter, or "whirlybird," as it was called. It became another angle, or photographic platform, from which Margaret took pictures. The whirlybird hovered over a scene while Margaret recorded, for *Life*, such views as sightseers poking their heads out of the crown of the Statue of Liberty and crowds of people at a Coney Island beach. A memorable photograph taken this way was of snow geese flying over a Virginia bay.

A three-year-old behind the barbed wire of her shantytown home; Johannesburg, South Africa, 1950

On this road she chose, of ever-escalating external excitement, she went to Korea in 1952. A war between North and South Korea, in which the United States and the United Nations played roles, had been in progress for a couple of

"EYES LIKE THE EAGLE"

years. She stopped off in Tokyo on her way and was in a station wagon shooting pictures of a May Day demonstration when her car was stoned. She was caught in the midst of a violent outbreak between police and students. Only when she could no longer see out of eyes streaming with tear gas did she give up shooting her pictures.

In an automobile which was stoned during a demonstration; Tokyo, Japan, 1952

From Tokyo she flew to Korea and worked on her story about the Korean people and, in particular, about communist guerrilla strongholds behind U.S. lines.

But something was happening to Margaret, something she would not admit to herself. She was having trouble getting in and out of jeeps, and her hands were stiffening on the camera. There was also a dull ache in her left leg and arm.

THE TOUGHEST ASSIGNMENT

She had called herself "Maggie the Indestructible," for she had never been seriously sick in her life. She had taken for granted her excellent health and agile body that responded to her needs like a perfectly tuned instrument. The sudden stiffening of her joints made her stagger. To cover up her awkwardness, because it embarrassed her, she thought up devices to gain time. She would pretend she had dropped something, perhaps a pencil, and would bend down to retrieve it. This gave her a few extra minutes during which she would regain her ability to walk.

For a while she continued with her work. But colleagues noticed her difficulties. Someone had to help her out of a car, and when she framed a picture in her camera, some-

Margaret's daily workout, stretching and exercising to keep limber

one else had to snap the shutter. Within a year her joints became increasingly stiff and her hands began to tremble.

The medical diagnosis of Margaret's symptoms was Parkinson's disease. Parkinson's is crippling and incurable, leading to increased stiffening of muscles and joints, tremor, and garbled speech. When Margaret learned the diagnosis, her life underwent swift and dramatic changes. She put every bit of her energy, ingenuity, and perseverance into conquering the illness.

She had made her home in Connecticut a haven. Even in her busiest years, she had restored her psychic energy and inner peace in the quiet countryside. Often she had spread a blanket outdoors on a bed of leaves and fallen

In retirement at her Connecticut home during the 1960's

asleep looking through tall trees at star-filled patches of sky. Now, too, during the early years of illness, she preferred to sleep outdoors in good weather. She would be made comfortable on a lounge near the pool and doze off to the sounds of insects and small animals scurrying through the grass. With her cat, Sita, keeping vigil, she was never lonely.

To combat the disease, Margaret twice underwent surgery. The procedures, still in the experimental stage, brought her moderate relief. She gained temporary control over her trembling hands, as well as some facility in movement. But only the most taxing, disciplined regimen of physical therapy kept her mobile.

She converted an open porch of her home into a miniature gymnasium where, with the help of a therapist, she did daily prescribed exercises. To keep her fingers flexible, she crumpled paper by the hour or wrung water out of towels. She did knee bends, played ball, and lifted weights. She danced the tango to maintain muscle coordination. Neighborhood children taught her how to play jacks and badminton and how to jump rope. Each day she walked one to three miles down the lanes and roads near her home, stopping to weed the ground around a cluster of wild columbine and jack-in-the-pulpit. Or she would stop to admire the mountain laurel and dogwood trees that filled the woods each spring with their delicate blossoms.

When she could no longer hold a pen in her hand, she learned to tap out words on a typewriter. That is how she worked on her autobiography, *Portrait of Myself*. When she could no longer sit at a typewriter, she had a tall table built and did her writing standing up. Though her last story for

Life appeared in 1956, the editors kept her name on the masthead until 1969 and promised Margaret the assignment to photograph the moon. Margaret had every hope that she would have recovered sufficiently to do so, as if her force of will could overcome her illness.

Her spirit in fighting Parkinson's won her as many laurels as had her extraordinary life as a photographer. "If I had to be ill," she remarked, "I was glad it was an illness I could do something about. I researched it as if it were another photographic assignment." She addressed groups of people with the same illness to encourage them by her example. She attended social functions, traveled, and went to dances. She always looked beautiful, whether her white hair was shorn down to her scalp, as it was after surgery, or whether she wore it long and full. Even when her body was beginning to stoop, she wore fetching gowns. But more than physical beauty enhanced her. Her excitement about life never wavered and her eyes, to the very end, mirrored her enthusiasm for every scene. Outside her windows she would see the daily panorama of nature unfold. At times, when the stiffness in her fingers eased, she took photographs of her cats, her friends, and neighborhood children. She had another weapon: "If you banish fear nothing terribly bad can happen to you," she told a newspaper interviewer.

Honors and awards multiplied. They had come her way from her first years as a photographer when, in 1928, one of her steel pictures won first prize in a Cleveland Museum of Art photography show. She was also celebrated for her daring exploits. Even the comic books made her a heroine. "The World's Most Famous Photographer Was a Girl," featured an issue of *Real Facts Comics*. The War Department handed her a citation; she picked up honorary degrees from universities, won an American Woman Achievement Award, and was elected to the Woman's Hall of Fame. In 1959, the Overseas Press Club held a dinner dance called "Peggy's Night" to celebrate her recovery from surgery. In 1960, a television movie based on her life featured movie star Theresa Wright in the lead role. Millions of viewers learned about Margaret's battle against her illness.

Colleagues and friends, who visited often, brought along packages of her favorite food and prepared special dishes for her. Margaret looked forward especially to visits by Alfred Eisenstaedt and Carl Mydans, *Life* colleagues. She missed her sister, Ruth, who died in 1964 (their mother had died many years before). Ruth, always loving and warm, had helped her with her books, reading the manuscripts and making valuable editorial suggestions. Her brother, Roger, and his family came from the Midwest where they lived to see her, and her cousin Robert Connolly and his family visited from New Jersey. "What a beautiful person she was," said her cousin sometime later. "She never complained."

In June, 1971, Margaret attended the fiftieth reunion of her high school graduation class. Accompanied by her companion of many years, Mrs. Marge Russell, she was driven to the country club in Plainfield, New Jersey. She was helped from the car into a wheelchair. By then she could talk only in a loud whisper. She greeted each classmate by name. "Hello, Jack," she said to her old co-editor of the high school magazine, John Daniel, whom she had not seen in fifty years. She spoke to him about his work in the ministry.

She fondly inquired about all those absent from the gathering.

Two months later, in August, 1971, she died.

She left behind a monumental body of work, so alive and telling, so filled with her visual artistry, that it reinvokes the brilliant woman. The camera, which had become an extension of her, led her on great adventures. At the same time, she stretched the scope of the camera and made it more meaningful, more responsive to her vision.

Even at the peak of her artistry, said photographer Alfred Eisenstaedt, Margaret Bourke-White was as willing and eager as any person on a first assignment. "She would get up at the crack of daybreak to photograph a bread crumb if necessary." For millions of people she documented and illuminated the historic events of twenty-five years: U.S. industry, the Great Depression, Soviet industrialization, wars and revolutions, and the human condition. She left not only a visual record of history but a written record as well. Her

Edward A. Steichen, photographer and friend, with Margaret at an earlier time

books, illustrated with her compelling photographs, still convey the drama of major events.

She had love and appreciation not only for the big things of the age. She maintained, until the end, her love for everything in nature.

Her friend Sean Callahan visited her in the hospital toward the end of her life. On the way in, he noticed a praying mantis on a bush. He picked it up and put it into an empty bottle. At Margaret's bedside, he held up the bottle for her to see his gift. She was by then almost completely paralyzed and had lost all power of speech. But Callahan had worked out with Margaret a form of communication through the blinking of her eyes. After a brief visit Callahan prepared to leave and bid her good-bye, leaving the praying mantis behind on her night table. He noticed that Margaret seemed fretful, and through the activity of her eyes he understood what she wanted him to do. Her last message was that he take the praying mantis outdoors and release it—so that it could be free.

Praying mantis by Margaret Bourke-White

THE TOUGHEST ASSIGNMENT

SELECTED BIBLIOGRAPHY

BOOKS BY MARGARET BOURKE-WHITE

Eyes on Russia. New York: Simon and Schuster, 1931.
U.S.S.R. Photographs. Albany, New York: The Argus Press, 1934.
(with Erskine Caldwell) *You Have Seen Their Faces.* New York: The Viking Press, 1937.
(with Erskine Caldwell) *North of the Danube.* New York: The Viking Press, 1939.
(with Erskine Caldwell) *Say, Is This the U.S.A.?* New York: Duell, Sloan and Pearce, 1941.
Shooting the Russian War. New York: Simon and Schuster, 1942.
They Called It "Purple Heart Valley." New York: Simon and Schuster, 1944.
"Dear Fatherland, Rest Quietly." New York: Simon and Schuster, 1946.
Halfway to Freedom. New York: Simon and Schuster, 1949.
(with John La Farge) *A Report of the American Jesuits.* New York: Farrar, Straus and Cudahy, 1956.
Portrait of Myself. New York: Simon and Schuster, 1963.

PUBLISHED PHOTOGRAPHS IN:

The Cornell Alumni News, December 23, 1926; January 13 and 20; February 10; May 19; June 2 and 23; September 29, 1927.
Fortune, February 1930 to October 1937.
Life, November 1936 to May 1956.
P.M. June 1940 to December 1940.

ALSO:

Brown, Theodore M. *Margaret Bourke-White, Photojournalist,* Andrew Dickson White, Museum of Art, Cornell University, 1972.
Callahan, Sean, ed. *The Photographs of Margaret Bourke-White,* New York Graphic Society, 1972.
Margaret Bourke-White, The Cleveland Years 1927-1930. The New Gallery of Contemporary Art, Cleveland, Ohio, 1976.

I found these materials invaluable to my research. They are for adults, but an interested reader might want to look them over in the library.
B.S.

INDEX

119

PHOTOGRAPH CREDITS

The estate of Margaret Bourke-White: jacket (Oscar Graubner), pp. 7, 8, 9, 11, 24, 54, 62, 83, 89

Syracuse University, The George Arents Research Library (by permission of Roger B. White): pp. ii, 2, 5, 6, 34, 41 (Ralph Steiner), 42, 44, 47, 72, 77, 96, 108, 110, 112

LIFE magazine, Time Incorporated: The Time-LIFE Syndication Service is the sole agent for the following photographs appearing in this book. pp. 60, 65, 69, 78, 84, 88, 94, 99, 101, 105, 107, 117

Cornell University, Herbert F. Johnson Museum of Art: pp. 18

Magnum Prints, Incorporated: pp. 116

The Museum of Modern Art Collection (by permission of Roger B. White): pp. 51, 55

The National Archives: pp. 40

The New Gallery of Contemporary Art, Cleveland, Ohio (by permission of Roger B. White): pp. 30

US Army: pp. 93

The Witkin Gallery, Incorporated: pp. 75

Courtesy of Bernard Hayden, Bound Brook, New Jersey: pp. 14

The photographs on the following pages were taken by Margaret Bourke-White: pp. 18, 30, 34, 40, 47, 51, 54, 55, 60, 62, 69, 77, 78, 84, 88, 94, 99, 101, 105, 107, 117